Reward System

Reward System

Jem Calder

faber

First published in 2022
by Faber & Faber Ltd
Bloomsbury House,
74–77 Great Russell Street
London WC1B 3DA

Typeset by Faber & Faber Ltd
Printed and bound by CPI Group (UK) Ltd, Croydon, CR0 4YY

The right of Jem Calder to be identified as author of this work
has been asserted in accordance with Section 77 of the Copyright,
Designs and Patents Act 1988

*This is a work of fiction. All of the characters, organisations,
and events portrayed in this novel are either products of the
author's imagination or are used fictitiously.*

A CIP record for this book
is available from the British Library

ISBN 978–0–571–36378–0

2 4 6 8 10 9 7 5 3 1

For my parents

Contents

A Restaurant Somewhere Else

Guess What

At the beginning of a December fifty-seven harvests prior to the Food and Agriculture Organization of the United Nations' projected start date for the era of total global soil infertility, Julia got the job at Cascine.

She called the closest person she had in her life, who was her mother, to deliver the news by voice.

'I can't believe it.'

'I know.'

'You'll be—'

'I know.'

'It's such a step *up*.'

'I know.'

'Such a step *forward*.' Her mother laughed, then kept laughing. 'Imagine that.'

The low-fidelity audio of her mother's laughter bade Julia to laugh as well. Their laughs were identical in cadence and dissimilar in pitch. Julia raised her non-smartphone-wielding hand to her head. 'I'm imagining.'

Late November

Throughout her three unpaid trial shifts, Julia had received orientative and procedural supervision from Lena, the sous-chef whose position the former would, after having successfully demonstrated her utility to the latter, eventually be hired to inherit.

'Mind your elbows.' 'Cut against the grain.' 'Sumac lives in the storeroom, not on the sideboard.' 'Next time, bring your own knife roll.'

Of the many formed and as-yet-unformed thoughts Julia had about Lena, the majority were dedicated to either comparing or deliberately attempting not to draw comparisons between their common and contrasting qualities. Lena was approximately Julia's goal weight and sported the kind of pixie cut that made women of lesser confidence ideate over cutting their own hair short. She could not have been any more than five years older than Julia, but the extent of her culinary proficiency suggested decades of experience separating them. Each time Julia left Cascine following a trial shift, she felt inadequate in some new way and certain it had been her last.

After what would in fact prove to be Julia's final trial shift, she and Lena exited the restaurant together into an unobtrusively warm front of glossy rain, leaving Ellery, the kitchen's head chef, to finish locking up by himself.

4

Outside, as they walked, Lena announced that she intended to endorse Julia to Ellery for the sous position. Julia thanked her so much, said oh my god oh my god she couldn't believe it, asked what were Lena's plans and where was she headed, and – although she'd been referring more to the short-term when she'd asked those questions – responded encouragingly when Lena replied, 'Somewhere good, Berlin, I have a connection out there.' Looking down, Lena performed an incisive task on her smartphone and added, in a modulated tone that made what she said sound like a sideways way of saying some-thing else, 'Yeah, I've just been here too long, I think.'

If she ever cut her hair as short as Lena's, Julia knew, she'd only want it long again after. She understood that all she really wanted was a change.

Because she was nice, Julia waited kerbside with Lena beneath the coldening rain, long enough for Ellery to catch up with and call goodnight to them both from his collapsible bike, its wheels raising a light spray as they planed the cycle lane's slicked surface. Shortly thereafter, Lena took her place among the city's Uber ridership and Julia never saw her again.

The Imitator

Julia spent her first days at Cascine imitating what little she'd known of Lena's presence there: emulating her easy familiarity with the chefs de cuisine; acting out the memory of her command over utensils.

In those earliest shifts, Julia felt – or felt as though she felt – the rest of the restaurant's mostly male staff mentally adding and subtracting competency and attractiveness points to and from their fluctuating impressions of her, tallying up opinions relating to her appearance and character which, once formed, would be hard for her to ever improve upon.

At her previous restaurant of employ – the latest in a series of incorporated dining ventures executively co-managed by a celebrity chef known, in the industry, for the emotionally toxic atmospheres of his kitchens and increasingly, on the industry's outside, for his strongly worded online free-speech punditry and resultant new-media fan base of neoconservatives – Julia had earned a reputation as an easy mark; a line chef overeager about the job and therefore manipulable into assuming responsibilities occasionally beneath, but more often than not well above, her pay grade.

She had been waiting to become the next version of herself at a new job for a long time, long months. She had to

6

be careful, now she was here, not to fall back into old-Julia behaviours: not to reveal her true nature as a crier, pleaser and worrier; not to do or say the kinds of things the person she was pretending to be wouldn't say or do. Not to let others' views of her warp her view of herself. Not to be vulnerable in the places she had been before.

The Apartment

After her first full week of non-trial shifts, Julia returned home to be airily 'Oh, hey'-ed by Margot – her landlord, flatmate, and older sister's closest friend – who was lying in her ritual night-time position on the living-room sofa; her attention split-screened between her smartphone's various feeds and an episode of prestige television streaming on her laptop.

The living room was moodlit in accordance with Margot's preferred rotary dimmer setting, thirty degrees clockwise from exact midway, as demarcated by a Sharpied dot on the white plastic casing of the wall's light switch.

'How's it going?' Julia replied.

Margot leant awkwardly over to pause her show. 'Oh, good. I'm just tired. How about— How's things with you?'

'Also good. Also tired. But good-tired. From the new job.'

'Oh yeah. How's it all—?'

'Good so far. *Very* good so far.'

Usually if she arrived back in the evening and saw, from the hallway, the telltale Margot-signalling band of light running beneath the living-room door, Julia would head immediately to bed. She and Margot had not yet worked out a natural, non-strained way to communicate with one another; their relationship was probably permanently contaminated by the monthly standing-order payments Julia transferred to her for rent.

'Better than the old place?'

'Oh god, like, about a zillion times better,' Julia said, the act of speech becoming increasingly wearying for her to perform.

'That's good. I'll have to stop by and try it sometime.'

'You must.'

'I will.'

'Cool. Well, goodnight.'

Margot reverted her attention to her devices. 'Goodnight.'

Winter Menu

Aside from maybe occasionally feeling left out of certain in-jokes and references whose origins predated her tenure there, Julia slotted quickly into place in the restaurant's small culture. The staff members who usually made those in-jokes were Ellery and Nathan, Cascine's fore- and second-most senior chefs respectively, whom Julia liked and who also seemed to like her back.

How the kitchen's chain of operations went was: Ellery and Nathan oversaw the hot section, while Julia and one or maybe two members of a high-turnover workforce of junior cooks alternated between the cold and prep lines. Occasionally she'd cover the plancha or assist on sauté, other times she'd work the pass and triage the incoming checks. (Ellery would always be the one to micromanage the presentations of the outgoing plates to which those checks corresponded – a responsibility he took pride in never delegating.)

When Ellery spoke to her directly or gave her pointers, she made sure to active-listen, nodding and saying things like, 'Okay, Chef,' or 'Got it, Chef,' which was overserious, probably; she should learn to relax around him. (On the occasions that it happened, her face flushed at hearing its wearer's name spoken in praise – Ellery looking at her with one eye closed, sighting her down the straight of his fork, 'Perfect texture, Julia,' having tasted her first-attempt youvetsi lamb stew.) Mainly, she just tried to work hard and keep her head down. To be seen simply as a safe pair of hands.

Rules

Ellery had a lot of rules, which he took pleasure in recounting larghetto and with irony, as if quoting from a list he'd long ago asked Julia to commit to memory and that she'd failed him in since having forgotten: no smartphones in the kitchen; no haircuts before a shift; no unironed T-shirts; black plastic utility clogs only; stick to your station (or its variant: disturb the mise, disturb the peace); no smartphones in the kitchen; if you're walking behind someone, say so; sanitise, sanitise, sanitise; did he mention no smartphones in the kitchen.

However annoyingly they were dictated, the rules at least prompted rare moments of collective discussion among the working chefs (Julia, who had never once taken her smartphone into the kitchen, suspected Ellery of deploying the rules primarily as icebreakers to shatter the extended silences that sometimes set in during peak labour hours); Nathan usually responding by citing instances of Ellery's violation of his own rules' basic precepts in objection; Ellery, in turn, responding to Nathan's responses by gesturing as though jacking off a thickly girthed, invisible dick – a routine that reliably, if a little forcedly, did make Julia laugh, and which she increasingly felt the two of them performed solely for that reason.

Rota

Given that she'd only recently been hired, Julia felt uncomfortable about requesting annual leave from the restaurant. This was a problem, because back when she'd first accepted the job, her mother had FaceTimed specifically to ask her to please, please book some time off so they could spend a couple of weeks at home together over the Christmas period – which Julia, knowing how lonely her mother sometimes got, had sworn she'd definitely do, fully in the knowledge, even as she'd made it, that she would not fulfil her promise.

Historically, the main way Julia dealt with conflicts in her life was to endlessly defer making any real decision or committing to any specific course of action, preferring instead to allow fate to autopilot her toward its natural-seeming, predestined outcomes without risking incurring any accidental negative consequences as a result of her own personal interference.

But out of sheer accumulated guilt for having raised her mother's hopes unduly, a week and a half before Christmas, Julia eventually did ask Ellery about taking some unexpected short-term holiday, to which he replied that he honestly wouldn't normally do this, that he was ordinarily mostly pretty lax about these things, but with the last days of December and first days of January tending to be so busy, he couldn't allow her to take any more days off than the few she'd already been auto-assigned on the restaurant's Google Sheets rota.

'Is that going to be okay?' he said, reframing as a question what had moments before been a series of clear declarations. And Julia, internalising shame, responded: 'Yeah totally, no worries, no definitely. Completely cool and fine.'

Stephanie

One late-afternoon communal lunch break, Julia was trying to talk to Stephanie, Cascine's head waiter, about her life and the things in it. Stephanie was putting little to no effort into the conversation and asking an unequal number of return-questions, acting cool and aloof in a way that forced the counterposition of tryhard oversharer onto Julia. The interaction had begun to feel – for them both – like a kind of test.

'And so, have you been here a long time?'

'Since I finished my PhD. About eight months.'

'Wow. And, were you studying around here before that, or?'

'Yeah.'

'That's amazing,' Julia said, then felt the words *that's amazing* expanding in dead air. 'Same here, I studied geography.'

'Oh right.'

'Yeah, MA not PhD. Human geography. I did four years. My dissertation was about how, gradually, soil—'

'And now you're a chef.'

'Yeah. Actually, it's a funny story—'

'I'll bet.'

Nightcap

After clearing the board and sending out the night's last cover, usually sometime around ten, Julia would seat herself on one of the tall swivel stools lining Cascine's semicircular bar area and call in the next day's wholesale order to its stockist's overnight voicemail service.

According to custom, Stephanie or whoever else was tending bar that night would pour Julia a post-service glass of house wine or mix her a cocktail using a low-markup spirit – a gesture of hospitality that was extended to every member of staff working the closing shift. Julia, a known lightweight whose sleep quality could be diminished by the imbibing of just half a beer, never wanted to drink after a service, but wanted even less to exclude herself from a collective workplace ritual by not drinking, and so accepted the offer with thanks every time.

Julia believed no one had noticed that she only ever mimed drinking in these situations (raising and lowering

13

her glass to and from her lips without taking a proper sip),
until, after observing this ruse for several nights running,
Stephanie called her out on it.

'Hey, if you're just going to pretend to drink your drink
like always, the least you can do is give it to Nathan.'

'What?' Julia said, eyes aimed downward; her defen-
sive reflex always to feign misunderstanding.

'What what?' Stephanie said, signalling to Julia's G&T.
'If you don't like the drinks I make for you, just give them
to someone else.'

Gingerbread

'Well, how's business?'

'Oh, I'm just doing this and that. The house is empty,
but soon it'll have you in it! For a whole two weeks!'

'Right. About that, Ma.'

'Oh, what, Jewel?' her mother said, disappointment-
inflecting her vowels.

After they'd finished talking, Julia continued with the
task she'd been performing prior to her mother's call. She
impressed the cutter into the biscuit dough, and cut out
the shape of a man.

Days

The part she liked most about working was also the part she was best at: tightening the outlet of her concentration around a specific object or task so that nothing else entered her attentional field; deep monotasking to the point of pure immersion in the deed – or set of deeds – at hand. Hours passed easily, like minutes, this way, her body all but detached from the experience of time; cooking faster than she could think, acting on gut feeling and motor skill without room for hesitation; her focus centred on, say, skimming a surface foam of whey from a Pyrex jug of clarifying butter, trimming a foreleg of Iberian ham into perfect featherweight slices.

Not really, but: sometimes she imagined the restaurant as a machine she stepped inside that processed the formless material of her days into units of consistent shape and texture.

Not really, but: sometimes she literally thanked actual God she'd gotten out of her previous job when she had.

Perspective

Because he'd seen her looking at it a couple of times, Nathan felt obliged to explain his forearm tattoo to Julia. It was a line-art inking of a see-through geometric cube,

15

drawn in such a way as to accommodate two possible interpretations of the shape's exact position in space, depending on which of the cube's square faces the viewer imagined was its frontal one; an optical illusion, he authoritatively informed her, that represented 'perspective'.

The Clementine

Julia, Ellery and Nathan were locking up the restaurant together.

Julia disposed of the mixed recycling and general waste, then stood outside, getting air. She flexed open and closed her hands just to feel them, gloveless in the winter night. Recently, the cold weather had been making her sad in a seasonal-affective way. After she'd had enough air she went back inside.

Ellery was leaning next to the doorway, paring the rind from a clementine using both his thumbnails while Nathan was setting an overnight alarm in the back office.

As Julia passed him, Ellery raised the clementine to occupy her visual field more fully. 'Want?' he said.

'Sure,' she said.

He tore the fruit into halves, and handed her the larger hemisphere.

Size Eight

'Thanks, Ma,' Julia said. 'I love it.' She looked at the gift, and then down at herself. She wondered whether the thing she wanted to say would dampen her mother's festive mood. 'I do worry, lately, that I've maybe put on some winter weight.'

Without pause, her mother concurred: 'You're a lot bigger than you once were.'

Julia let her hands, and the Peter-Pan-collar dress that occupied them, sink into the sheet of deluxe glassine tissue paper from which she had extracted the gift. 'Great, Ma.'

Her mother's face drew into a hangdog expression. 'Don't be upset with me on Christmas. You know I didn't mean that mean.'

Difficulty

Owen – a junior chef de cuisine whom Julia had already had to reprimand twice on separate days for failing to rotate older stock to the fronts of the fridges after being directly asked to do so – was having difficulty gelatinising-without-burning the white roux that would act as both base and thickening agent for that evening's béchamel sauce.

'Watch me do this closely,' Julia said, taking over Owen's position behind the burner and commandeering

17

his equipment, 'because I'm only going to do it once.'

She dialled down the heat using the range's frontal console to prevent any rendered fat from burning against the inside of the cast-iron pan containing Owen's roux-in-progress; 'You have to keep up the momentum, or else it'll caramelise,' she narrated, demonstrating the best way to exert a consistent level of torque over the whisk in one's hand; 'it's fiddly, but keep your elbow nice and steady,' all movement originating from the wrist's axis of rotation; stirring in a circular, clockwise motion, 'like so,' in volutions of gradually expanding-then-contracting circumference; chunks of flour beginning to solubilise and assimilate into the custard-viscosity fluid.

After further reducing the heat, she rested the whisk against the rim of the pan, then continued motioning her hand in the air, as if still stirring. 'Y'see?'

'I see.'

Before she returned to her own duties, she hesitated near Owen for a moment longer, granting him an extended opportunity to thank her, which he didn't take.

I Feel Like Today Has Been Really Short

Owen was prone to making jejune observations relating to the day's perceived length or long-windedly recapping things he'd seen online in ways that Julia inwardly could not stand but outwardly always felt it her duty to respond to with equivalently lightweight phrases such as, 'Oh yeah, that *is* weird,' so he didn't feel ignored. The cumulative effect of all her niceness was that she liked him a lot less than any of her other colleagues.

Mornings

Her routine was to wake in the dawn's faint, rose-coloured light, purchase a flat white and an icing-sugar-dusted cinnamon bun from the third-wave coffee shop near her apartment where the baristas remembered her order but never her name and with whom she sometimes exchanged reassuringly formal remarks about the weather, and to interchange, outside, from roadside pavement to green-space footpath, taking the scenic route through the common-land park that lay before Cascine, maybe pausing to witness the dispersal and regrouping of a helix of migratory starlings or else a chevron of Canada geese before exiting the park alongside a private nursery school whose front gate would, on weekdays, already at that early hour be flanked by its first rotation-duty detail of nightstick-armed guards, all the while systematically consuming the comestibles she held, one in each hand, as concomitantly as she could in a carefully synchronised, probably ugly-to-look-at bite/sip/ bite/sip rhythm she'd devised to occupy her mouth with as much of the two simultaneous tastes as possible, believing, as she did, that each individual foodstuff was best enjoyed in concert with the other – the background milkiness of the coffee intensifying the sweetness of the cinnamon bun; every additional chew of the pastry's leavened crust inciting further demand for the coffee's dampening effect – repeating the alternating bite/sip process until both nutriments were depleted and she was left, sated, with a fully compostable cinnamon-bun-perspiration-blotted napkin in one hand and an empty, only semi-biodegradable coffee cup in the other.

Julia Doesn't Smoke

Nathan headed outside to smoke and asked Julia if she wanted to join, waving, in her direction, an olive-green pack of debranded cigarettes.

Julia stood absorbing the offer for a moment and pictured becoming a smoker: taking breaks; borrowing lighters; administering to herself an addiction for the sake of being able to satisfy it – perhaps to yield further satisfactional dividends down the line by eventually quitting. She smiled weakly at Nathan and said, 'I'm fine.'

Ellery Says

Ellery says taste is the body's slowest sense. Most times you'll have swallowed your whole mouthful by the time you capture an impression of its flavour, only to be returned, a moment later, back to the feeling of never having tasted anything at all.

Survivor's Guilt

During the lull before the dinner rush, they were talking about a friend of Ellery's who'd died a year ago to the day. He had been thirty-three.

'How'd he die? I always have to know when they die young.' She felt ashamed to have sounded so enthused. 'Sorry.'

'That's okay. He hung himself.'

'I'm sorry.'

'With a bungee cord. At his parents' house.'

'Sorry.'

Ellery would someday describe to Julia a strong yet difficult-to-exactly-name feeling he sometimes felt – an emotion that stalked him from the past and occasionally caught up with him in the present if he stayed too still or thought the wrong sequence of memories. 'I think his dad found him. He had a bad drug problem and he couldn't figure it out, so.

21

I guess at a certain point he just knew his life wasn't going to get any better – like he might have better days ahead of him, but no real good ones. That's opiates for you. So.'

Julia Overhears Ellery Talking to Stephanie About His Brain

'When you're basically an addict for a decade like I was – when you do so much drugs over so long a period of a time – your brain literally physically rewires to accommodate all the extra stimulus and all the, like, surplus dopamine you're crowding it with. But what that means is, when you have withdrawals, your brain isn't just running dry, there's actually physically *more dry* for your brain to run than with most other people's brains? Because of how many extra, like, dopamine receptors your reward system or whatever has grown to keep up with all the excess, like, gratification you've been inputting it with? So eventually, all those extra receptors you've been depending on to have a good time have to die off. And when that happens – well, basically – you'd pretty much rather die yourself.'

Ellery Breathes

Working in such close proximity to Ellery, the nose-breathing became a problem. The dog-whistle-pitch, circular in-and-out sound; loud enough, given the kitchen's limited square footage, to remain audible no matter which of its workstations you stood behind; the dissonant noise at irreconcilable odds with every other noise you heard.

Sometimes Julia found herself hours deep into visualising the anatomical structure of Ellery's inner nose; became borderline obsessed with trying to mentally map the size and shape of his septum and sinuses – airways likely eroded by a decade-plus of intranasal drug abuse.

Other times, she might, as a game, try to match the metre of her own nose-breathing to his, or let herself get so annoyed by the sound as to be able to extract a kind of inverse gratification from it.

The depth and therefore volume of his tidal respirations, Julia noticed, increased the longer he stayed engaged in any single given task. In time, she learned to accommodate the annoyance.

The Celebrity

Some evening, a recognisably famous television presenter/ fashion designer/model/author came for dinner at Cascine. She was wearing a sandstone-coloured cap of the same workwear brand as Ellery's favourite winter jacket, Stephanie reported, and was seated at table three in the company of a non-famous but above-averagely attractive male.

Ellery, Nathan and Owen all took long glances at the celebrity, one by one authenticating the validity of Stephanie's surveillance, sharing in the contact high of being proximal to someone of such stardom. Nathan remarked on how jarringly accustomed he felt to seeing the celebrity's face – said something to the effect that having been exposed to her likeness for so long and across so wide an array of media made the experience of seeing her in real life feel comparable to déjà vu. Owen bashfully agreed, silently recalling a time when, years ago – in the spirit of experimentation – he'd masturbated to pictures of the celebrity's feet.

Julia, who in working the pass that evening was afforded the best view of the front-of-house in the entire rest of the house, felt proud of herself for not looking at the celebrity, and doubly proud of herself for not drawing attention to the fact that she hadn't looked at the celebrity.

Though she would never have said it aloud, and would especially not say it now, she had always felt a special connection to the celebrity – had in fact for years harboured the belief that they were similar in some private and profound way, their personalities linked by a deep commonality of essence.

When the celebrity's main course was ready to be served – a hissingly hot pork sisig served Pinoy-style beneath a raw egg – Julia took extra care to ensure the meal's presentation

24

was beautiful. Deftly, she rubbed the inside of her mouth with the tip of her forefinger and, using that finger as a kind of swab, introduced trace quantities of her salivary DNA into the celebrity's meal.

For the next hour, Julia felt the celebrity's presence haunting the vague, colourless margins of her thoughts and vision.

Late in the evening, unable to help it any longer, she convinced herself that pointedly ignoring the celebrity was basically equally as rude as looking right at her. So she looked.

Ellery's Name

Julia remembered the first time, just under two months ago, she'd heard Ellery's name out loud – 'Rhymes with celery' – how alien it'd sounded before repeat usage patterned it into something familiar, supplanting whatever thought had previously occupied the name's space in her mind, becoming a word that sometimes just occurred to her out of the blue.

Ellery's Body

Ellery was six-foot-something: tall enough that he had to hunch in a way he sometimes complained about to use the kitchen's stainless-steel work surfaces; broad enough that his physical volume appreciably diminished the available space of most rooms he entered; possessor of square shoulders, a cereal-coloured crew cut that connected with some same-coloured, carefully kempt facial hair, and the all-purpose confidence of a man accustomed to being well liked.

Age-, looks- and personality-wise, Ellery was not the type of guy Julia would usually be into – was perhaps even the type of guy she'd normally actively avoid – but a reduced sample size of other men in her life (given that most of her nights and weekends were spent in the kitchen) had occasioned a kind of selection bias that weighted his presence with perhaps otherwise unmerited statistical significance. Although she herself didn't find Ellery especially attractive, Julia could imagine finding him attractive if she simultaneously imagined being a slightly older and more confident type of woman – someone Lena-like – which from time to time she did find herself imagining.

As if too frequent contemplation of the desires of others had rewired those of her own, within three weeks of first having had this thought, Julia found herself unable to think about much other than if Ellery ever thought about fucking her. It wasn't like there was a lot else to think about in the enforced intimacy of the very cramped, very temperate space in which they both performed their very physically demanding jobs; wilfully or not, the thought must, at some point, have crossed his mind.

But only on an evening in late January – watching Ellery bed a collar steak in toasted farro while she imagined his hands all over her – did she pause mid-fantasy to realise the full extent of the unplanned crush that she'd developed on him.

Ellery's Lightness of Touch

Cascine had opened five years earlier to positive reviews praising its concise, focused menu of small plates; obeyance of the natural patterns of seasonal produce cultivation; and absence of overt allegiance to any existing culinary genre, which succeeded in constituting a culinary genre all of its own.

Only one review Julia could find online made mention of Ellery by name. Multiple nights, before and after getting the job, she'd reread the review's few freely available paragraphs down to where it'd been paywalled off mid-sentence.

The section to which her thoughts most often returned, though, was the mystifying standfirst that ran atop the webpage in semibold-weight text: *'Cascine exudes an effortless atmospheric lightness, informed by its head chef's own lightness of touch.'*

On an afternoon in early February, Ellery entered the kitchen texting, artificial keystroke sounds issuing from his touchscreen device.

'I know I'm breaking my own rule,' he said, not looking up from his smartphone, 'but this is boring-logistical-family stuff, so it's allowed.' The device chimed and he murmured, but unmistakably did pronounce, the words: 'My daughter.'

Julia, determined not to overly involve herself in the personal-life conversations that sometimes occurred in the kitchen, couldn't believe that nobody was asking any follow-up questions concerning Ellery's never-before-mentioned daughter.

Three shifts later, after the night's final cover and in a painstakingly offhand tone affected to downplay the seventy-two hours she'd spent circulating the question in her head, she asked him: 'I'm sure you didn't, but did you say the other day you had a daughter?'

Ellery looked up from the prep sheet he was prepping longhand for the following morning. 'Did I what?'

'I said I'm sure you didn't' – she wished she'd started a shorter version of her question for its second time around – 'but did you say the other day you had a daughter?'

'Yeah,' Ellery said, in a factual, non-revelatory tone. He held up his obsolescent-model smartphone and activated its side button, tapping the picture of the late-teenaged girl that constituted its lock-screen – the screen's glass cracked enough for an inch-sized swatch of its underlying pixels to be permanently glitched out, distorting the girl's neck and upper torso into bluish fractals. 'That's her.'

Julia's Confidence

A side-effect of finding Ellery newly attractive was that her inhibitions were heightened in his presence. She experienced difficulty concentrating when they worked alongside one another – worrying about the jut of her nose as seen in profile, or, worse, when he stood behind her, the imagined sight of her own broad shoulders as viewed from the reverse.

One evening, when Nathan re-enacted the same physical comedy he did almost every closing shift with the bin bags, Julia, aware of being looked at by Ellery – and while pretending not to notice that she was the object of his gaze – found herself self-consciously unable to remember the sound of her normal laugh, and so faked an alarmingly loud, theatrical laugh in its place.

Afterward, embarrassed, and not wanting her face to lapse back into its default unattractive resting cast, she contorted her expression into a knowing half-smile that she hoped looked appealing to men in general and to Ellery in particular. She held the smile for as long as she remained conscious of her face.

The Celibate

Pretty celibate this whole past year, actually. With only a wall separating her from Margot and only a global-cellular-network connection separating Margot from her older sister (and not to mention with Margot having already complained several times, albeit in a passive-aggressive, roundabout way, about Julia's noisemaking when she came home late from work), Julia had been too sound- and space-conscious to bring any boys back to the apartment since moving in.

Except, actually, for the dispiriting night in maybe the previous March when Margot had been away staying with family and Julia had had over a nice enough, very affectionate guy she'd met at a bar. In the living room then her bedroom, they'd tried for a long time to have sex but he couldn't get it in, and, after several failed, very manual attempts to insert himself inside her, he'd said he'd like to leave. Julia had insisted that he please just stay, but the guy had insisted in a more serious tone of voice than the one she'd used that he'd really rather go.

When, a few days later, Julia had texted him a light-hearted observation relating to a joke he'd formerly made, she'd received no response. For months thereafter, upon future remembrance of the whole episode, she would murmur to herself, with her hand against her mouth: 'Oh god, oh god, oh god.'

Nathan Says

Nathan says the energy content in all foodstuffs can be traced back, through multiple processes of photosynthetic conversion, to – at source – some original harnessing of the sun's raw thermophotonic power; that every kilojoule of caloric energy is essentially just reconstituted solar force. The sun makes the plants grow, animals consume and extract the glucose stored inside those plants, humans consume those animals or else the plants themselves, etc.

Julia said that certainly sounded true, but she wasn't sure if it really was: 'You might be oversimplifying there, Nath.'

Ellery shook his head, unseen, and said nothing.

The Button

Many of them were gathered beneath a plexiglass smoking-section canopy which was itself beneath a gathering rain. They were listening to Nathan explain why he didn't believe in pressing the call button at traffic-light pedestrian crossings.

He accused the buttons of being placebos, emblematic of a culture-wide individualist fantasy, that bore no causal relation to the speeds of alternation between the signals they supposedly quickened, nor, by extension, to the flows of traffic governed by those signals – especially obvious, he went on, when one factored in other co-integrated network functions such as fixed-time public transport scheduling, or even momentarily considered the logistical implications behind operating an interconnected system of roadways whose circuitry had to accommodate the variable, many-and-all-at-once competing right-of-way demands of the city's entire motorist and pedestrian throughputs: 'It just makes no sense!' he cried.

Julia had been laughing hard the whole time Nathan had been speaking, and had also, at some point, managed for the back of her right hand to fall carefully into contact with Ellery's left. Not really, but: for a long time afterward, the small surface area of her body that had touched his radiated a lingering warmth.

Deep Clean

Sundays between services they deep-cleaned. Two hours spent exfoliating the restaurant's every flat surface, coughing on the astringent smells of the stockroom's various commercial-grade bleaches, canned aerosols, ten-litre drums of concentrated detergent gels.

Afterward, she would step outside to breathe deeply the cool, low-quality city air contaminated by microplastics, lead particulate, nitrogen and sulphur dioxides; the grey, early-evening sky above her gleaming or else just appearing to gleam like one endless, sterile, epoxy-resin kitchen floor.

The Keybearer

After two months at Cascine, Julia was inducted into the keybearers' club, meaning she was entrusted to open and lock up the restaurant by herself. Of the kitchen staff, only she, Ellery and Nathan possessed keys to the business, which, they stressed, was 'a profound and sacred honour'.

Halfway home after her first late shift closing up alone, Julia started to doubt whether she'd actually remembered to lock the restaurant's front door. Hooping her keychain around and around her forefinger as she walked, she was mostly pretty sure she had locked it, but, when she paused to recall the specific memory of having done so, she could only draw a blank.

Hours later, awake in bed, she still felt uncertain about having locked the door. She thought her way backwardly along the day's chain of events, but somehow the memory of locking up remained ungraspable.

Her doubts grew worse as the night wore on. Had she really forgotten something so essential? It wasn't the kind of error she'd usually make, but that didn't mean she hadn't made it now.

She definitely had held the keys in one hand and closed the door with the other – but had she definitely locked it? The harder she tried to remember the details, the blurrier they became.

She attempted sleep, even though the restaurant might be being burgled. She switched positions, even though she knew that, in the event of a robbery, having an unlocked door would void the restaurant's insurance. If anything happened overnight, it'd all be her fault. She checked her smartphone: her next shift began in under eight hours.

She slipped out of bed, dressed, and – avoiding the floorboards she knew would audibly complain – quietly left the apartment.

Outside, the night was so black it looked navy; the streets all mostly deserted. Just visible in the distance, the city's high-rise ranges were darkened as if on standby.

Door to door, Cascine was forty minutes' walk from her building – fifteen if she sped up the journey with a ten-minute bus ride, although that route only ran once hourly after midnight.

Striding as fast as she could, Julia felt embarrassed, like each occasional pedestrian she passed knew exactly what she was doing – her pace giving her away. The walk was cold and tense; at some point, she halted mid-step to frisk the outsides of her jacket and trouser pockets, fleetingly convinced she'd forgotten her keychain back at the apartment.

She hadn't, though, and as she crossed the park, hewing closely to its best-lit areas, she felt increasingly anxious about whatever scene she might encounter at the restaurant.

And when she finally arrived there, she placed both hands – then sighed, then leant her full bodyweight – against the door's locked handle.

The Governess Falls in Love With the Stablehand

Because she knew her mother didn't have many people to talk to in her life and that Wednesdays marked the remotest point of interspace between her Sunday fellowships at St Mike's, Julia made it a midweek habit to FaceTime with her during the breaks that divided her split shifts at the kitchen.

In their calls, they usually discussed hometown church gossip or goings-on at their workplaces; compared whatever sporadic updates they'd each received from Julia's sister – who had, since the previous summer, been away on a long, expensive-looking backpacking trip with her blandly handsome Canadian fiancé – before her mother wrapped things up by relaying the latest episodic plot synopses of the dense romantic sagas she read on her Kindle.

Nathan Raises a Concern Outside a Bar on His Birthday

'Yeah, y'know, what's dystopian is companies you haven't even provided your data to in exchange for services that you don't even use are shadow-profiling you. As in: they're able to construct a consumer outline of you using, like, user data they've collected secondhand – so, for instance, if your aunt or someone has uploaded her contacts list to some gambling website or wherever, from there they can, these companies, they can then proceed to track your entire internet presence just to market you, like, goods? Even though you haven't signed or filled out any privacy agreement or GDPR consent form or anything; once they gather all their invisible cloud-stored data and form an analytics-based, like, composite version of you, from then on you're being tracked. Which, like, supposedly it's totally opt-outable, this microtargeting, but in order to be able to opt out, you actually have to opt in to request that they delete your, like, proprietary information in the first place? So there's really no way to—? There's no regulatory— I don't know, sorry. I spend a lot of trime – a lot of *time trying* – to work this stuff out in my head. I watch a lot of videos. Oh man, Julia. If I imagine myself as you, hearing me saying all this, that's embarrassing. Sorry. I know you don't, uh— I just really like you. No, wait, listen. I just really like you so much and I know you don't like me the same way back and that's fine, I just wanted to let you know. I've seen the way you— I just thought I should say. Sorry, I'm— For a minute there I— I've really drunk a lot tonight. We can go back inside whenever. I didn't mean to offload all that onto you. Oh, fuck. Can't believe I'm—' He backhanded away his tears. '*Anyway*. Sorry. I just need a second to calm down. D'you think you could maybe wait out here with me while I calm down?'

The Storm

Microbeads of ultrafine February hail bit into the left side of Julia's face – its right she angled leeward from the oncoming wind on her walk toward Cascine.

By the time she arrived at work, a cold wave and resultant hurricane-force anticyclonic storm had descended upon the city: heavy beds of snowdrift were accreting outside; the roads had whited over long before nightfall.

The evening's reservations ended up being mostly all cancellations or no-shows; by close, a mere twenty covers had been served. Julia, Ellery and Stephanie were the only members of staff who remained at the restaurant for the whole late shift, which they completed as a skeleton crew, working through their routine chores aimlessly and with intermittent breaks to discuss the developing weather system outside.

From each of Cascine's street-facing windows, only amber-lit whisks of snowfall were visible, disturbed occasionally by the hurrying-past of phantom silhouette forms; shadow profiles.

'So, as soon as it snows, no one's hungry?' Ellery said to Julia – a joke she later heard him repeating to Stephanie.

Although no power cut had occurred, the relative quiet of the evening and blizzard-occluded outside view had the effect of making the restaurant feel somewhat blacked out and isolated, and therefore charged with partly scary, partly erotic potential.

'Does anyone else feel like drinking?' Julia said, considering now igniting some tealight candles to establish an ambiance.

'Honestly, I think we should probably lock up and get out of here,' Stephanie said, seemingly taking pleasure in being the night's voice of reason. 'Make sure we're all home safely.'

Julia Has Two Questions

After closing a few nights later – the unstable, easterly air mass since having dissipated and the last of the snow-melt now evaporating – they were heading together in the same direction toward neither of their homes. Ellery walked his bicycle between them, one hand supporting its handlebar's stem.

'Can I ask you a question?'

'It would seem' – he did a voice – 'you already have.' Their faces gained then lost legibility of expression as they passed through a conical shaft of streetlight. In the dark he said, 'Yes.'

'It's about not doing drugs.'

'Great,' he said.

'I guess I'm just interested in how—' She was unfamiliar with recovery and its relevant terms. 'I'm wondering why, if you're sober, and you know you've had problems with drugs and alcohol in the past, why is it you still drink sometimes?' She thought to say, then did say: 'Not that I think you're a bad drinker or anything.'

For a long time Ellery remained silent; must have been thinking. Not until they were within range of the next lamppost's halo of light could she differentiate his face from the night surrounding it.

Hours Later

Having walked in basically one big circle beginning and ending outside Cascine, they continued their night in a new, prohibitively expensive cocktail bar that they agreed they'd both ordinarily have avoided, but whose trading licence permitted the vending of alcohol until a later hour than at any of its neighbouring premises.

The more they got to talking, the more small and interesting ways Julia found the actual Ellery deviated from her impression of him. She was surprised to discover that many of his views coincided with her own: that he, like her, found the city's 'restaurant scene' affected and embarrassing; that he also had no opinion either way about people Instagramming their food; that he too had mixed feelings about his own religious upbringing.

They were leaning closely against one another, enjoying purer, more drawn-out versions of the incidental if sometimes lingering bodily and eye contact they'd previously made. Probably on account of a dopaminergic nervous response to a full night's drinking, but possibly also because what she felt was the real deal, when she kissed him she registered zero emotional traces of nervousness or uncertainty, only quiet in the wide-open spaces between her thoughts.

She hadn't felt she'd had to try – she reflected, ascending

the stairwell to her apartment after they'd said goodbye – nor that she'd even had a choice. Inevitable, as if the whole evening had been running on rails.

Where's Ellery?

'At the chiropractor,' Nathan said, 'getting a *massage.*' It was the first time since the night of his birthday they'd been alone together. To compensate, he was making more jokes than usual; he was anxious not to appear too anxious. 'So I'm in charge. And things are *really going to change around here*, my friend.'

'Oh great,' Julia said. She was relieved that he seemed not to want to acknowledge anything he'd said before.

'No more messing around on my watch.'

'Yes, Chef.'

'But seriously, though,' he called, as she headed through to the accessible bathroom to change into her whites, 'he'll be back this afternoon.'

Romantic Comedy

Ellery took Julia to one of Cascine's competitor restaurants that she'd heard a lot about but had never been inside. 'Think of it like a field trip,' he'd said ahead of time.

For the meal's full duration, her dress wouldn't leave

her alone: its elasticised sides continually rode up to a pinch point around her waist; its idiotic Peter Pan collar cloyed ceaselessly about her neck.

Sitting opposite Ellery with basically nowhere else to look other than right at him, she was beset by a nervousness she tried to overcome by speaking fast and gesticulating a lot. 'This is all so – like, so good. Was it you who told me they cook everything here using just induction heat?'

'Yeah.' Ellery had long ago learned that, to appear attractive, all he had to do was outrelax the person he was attempting to attract. 'Maybe.'

They consumed eight multiregional tasting-menu courses of progressively diminishing size – Ellery's favourite was a photogenic pork terrine plated with a dome of orange compote.

The bill took a long time to arrive after they'd requested it; Ellery, who believed the quality of a restaurant's service staff indicated something innate of the character of its management, said that such a laxity was typical of the business's owner, whom he knew personally and disliked.

Later, when they were walking together, Julia noted how highly Ellery spoke of his daughter; his superstitious avoidance of manhole-covering pavement slabs. At some point, she made a mutually deprecating joke about how her hands looked Ellery's age.

'I live not too far away from here,' he said in not-response. 'Do you want to come over for a gelato, or a wine, or—?'

A Gelato, or a Wine, Or

They Ubered from a street near the restaurant to Ellery's walkably close apartment. Standing in his living room, Julia wound a tress of hair around her forefinger and drew it under her nose and across her face; inhaled its organic, Julia-like smell.

From the kitchen, Ellery asked what would she like. He had nice wine if she wanted to try some, but he was afraid the gelateria was fresh out. She said sure to the wine, no worries about the gelato, and that his apartment was very grown-up.

'I am a grown-up, though,' he said, entering the living room with two empty glasses before returning to the kitchen then re-entering the living room with an opened bottle of wine.

'Do you have music?'

'Yeah, the laptop connects to the speaker, but. Keep it quiet.' He gestured in the direction of an interior wall and stage-whispered, 'The neighbours.'

They sat side by side on the living-room floor, between its sofa and coffee table. Julia woke Ellery's laptop and

43

asked for his password, which he declined to give – reaching, instead, across her waist to enter it himself. As he typed, she saw that his password was alphanumeric and began with an upper-case 'L'.

His desktop background was the operating system's default mountainscape one, and after she'd made fun of him for it, Julia launched his internet browser, navigated to YouTube and tried to think of something mood-appropriate to play. She settled on a copyright-infringing fan-uploaded fifty-one-minute video of the full Joni Mitchell album *Hejira*; the music visually accompanied by a slideshow of watermarked Getty images of Joni Mitchell that each Ken-Burns-effected before wiping offscreen.

Alongside the video, Julia noticed a sidebar of algorithmically recommended YouTube content, curated according to Ellery's historical viewing preferences. The videos suggested in the playlist had titles like: 'Twelve Simple Stretches for Chronic Back Pain', 'On Charisma and Getting the Women You Want', 'The Body Language of High Status Men' and 'College Professor Destroys Feminist Student'.

Unsure of whether to say anything about the videos or just ignore them, Julia averted her gaze from the laptop's screen and watched as Ellery poured two glasses of wine, then left them up on the coffee table to aerate.

He rotated the bottle in his hand and stared at its label for long enough to read it over twice. 'Y'know this wine is legit thirty years old?'

'Wow,' Julia said, trying not to imagine Ellery sitting alone in his apartment using the internet.

'Aren't you going to make a joke about how the wine's, like, half as old as me or something?'

'Oh, honestly I didn't even think to,' she said. 'But yeah, let's just imagine I did.'

'Well. Fuck you.'

She laughed and then fell quiet.

'You aren't exactly talkative a lot of the time. At work.'

'Yeah, well. I know.'

'I think the guys— I think Nathan and Owen—'

'What?'

'I think they're scared of you.'

Julia laughed again, but did understand what he meant. She was pleased he had said what he had said. 'Do I scare *you*?'

'No,' he said. 'Do *I* scare *you*?'

She thought around for a good answer before, finding none, she went with: 'No.'

Ellery headed to the bathroom, and while he was gone Julia stared at his laptop's dimmed, power-conserving display. She considered typing the first few letters of her name into his browser's address bar to see if it autocompleted with evidence that he'd looked her up online.

A moment later, she got jumpscared by the sound of Ellery's voice coming from directly behind her. 'I like this,' he said, walking around the room to face her, an index finger raised, referring to the music; it was unclear if he meant he'd heard *Hejira* before and enjoyed it, or if he was just now hearing and enjoying it for the first time.

'Shall we try the wine?' Julia said.

They delicately cheersed their glasses and Ellery said, 'Remember, you're drinking thirty years of history here.' Julia took a thin sip of thirty years of history and tasted multiple wars; economic recessions; iconic acts of terror; the rise of consumer electronics; Catholic school; kids are cruel; Accutane; learning to drive; meals every day; global ecological degradation; crying in the rain.

Partly because she wanted to but mostly because she felt it was due, that night Julia decided to sleep with Ellery. The whole thing was over before she could think too hard about it, and afterward they lay there being very nice with each other.

She had found ways to enjoy the experience – had liked saying the impromptu, pornography-appropriated things she'd said to him while he was inside her – and could already envision enjoying different variations on the night's same basic template in the future.

Lying with Ellery – the frontal plane of his body butted against the back of hers – and sharing in a specifically postcoital-calibre silence, she thought their encounter over and found she recollected it almost entirely out-of-bodily, as though she'd only been present watching them in the third person.

What she'd really wanted, she supposed, was for him to have lain heavily on top of her; to have borne down hard upon her with the fullness of his total weight. In reality, she wasn't sure if this was a real thing actual people did, or, if they did do it, how they might go about asking.

She felt like, after she'd slept, everything would reset back to normal by morning. And in the endmost blurry moments of confusion before her day-worn thoughts tapered off into abstractions then dreams, she became momentarily aware of – but would not later recall – a concentrative expression on her new bed partner's face, uplit, in blue, by his smartphone.

The Next Morning

When she awoke on what felt like the next morning but was actually just a later hour of the same morning on which she'd earlier fallen asleep, she lay for a while in a lateral position in semi-darkness in the otherwise empty bed, adjusting to her new surroundings and the placement

47

of objects in the unfamiliar room, nonlinearly remembering her memories of the previous night.

She checked her smartphone and read a recently delivered text from Ellery, then sat up and then lay down again before finally deciding to stand. That she was so disappointed Ellery had gotten up and gone to work already she took as an honest indicator of her feelings for him.

After assembling and donning the base layers of her last night's outfit, she called out 'Hello' and 'Ellery' a few times, then – satisfied she was definitely alone in the apartment – padded barefoot through to the cold, laminate-floored bathroom and curled out a shit that came out smooth and heavy as a hockey puck.

Later, leaving Ellery's building with wet hair and smelling of his bodywash, she decided to recap her night to someone else so as to make better sense of it herself. She thumbed through her smartphone's record of sent and received messages while considering to which of her contacts she most wanted to talk – stepping distractedly into and then immediately back out of the path of an oncoming motorcade of one-way traffic.

Teddy and Roos – the only university friends Julia had kept in touch with since moving to the city – came respectively first and second to mind. They each, she was pretty sure, lived in apartments that were relatively close to Ellery's; it'd be nice, since she was feeling sociable, to hang out with either one of them. She revolved in her head the idea of seeing Teddy, who loved to gossip and revel in the embarrassments of his friends, then the idea of seeing Roos, who was a better listener than Teddy but usually less prone to flattery in her opinions of Julia. Although, she then recalled, with an accompanying sensation of rapid-onset guilt, hadn't she allowed each of their most recent inbound texts to sit unanswered in her inbox for several (wincing, she checked the exact read-receipt dates as she walked) weeks, in Teddy's case, and, in Roos's case, *months*?

Still, it wasn't like she had any auxiliary friends to choose from – nor could she really discuss anything Ellery-related with anyone from Cascine. Vaguely alluding to having been super-busy with work lately, she texted Teddy and they arranged to meet in half an hour for coffee.

During that half-hour, the hangover Julia previously thought she'd somehow managed to avoid came over her in full – manifesting quadriphasically as a warming in her core temperature, then the sweats, then a headache, before settling on its final form as a bout of full-body nausea.

She regretted having texted Teddy and debated in her head over the etiquette of maybe now cancelling on him. By the time the pro-cancellation side of her brain had won out against the anti-cancellation side, she roused her smartphone while trying to come up with something

apologetic but also blameless she could say to excuse herself from their plans, only to discover that Teddy had
already messaged, confirming he was en route.

She arrived at the coffee place before he did and
secured a table as close to its front window as possible – the deeper into its seating area they sat, the longer
she felt like they'd stay. After she'd rehydrated on an
entire carafe's-worth of cucumber-infused tap water, she
noticed Teddy pulling on the push-to-open front door,
body-languaged to him that he needed to push it, and –
once they'd traded two very different-energy greetings
– had to think of a good response when he said, 'Hey,
you're all dressed up.'

'Actually it's: I'm *still* dressed up.'

Becoming aware of the specific friend-position he'd
been summoned to fulfil, Teddy said, 'Say more.'

'Okay. So.' She paused to formulate her next sentence
carefully, which had the unintentional storytelling conse-
quence of causing narrative tension to build; Teddy leant
in toward her. 'I had sex with my boss last night.'

Teddy made big eyes and said, 'And – you're okay with
that?'

'No. I mean yeah, I like him. I'm happy about it.'

'But I thought you said— Isn't he, like, some famous
racist?'

'No, I don't work there anymore.'

50

'Oh, right. Yeah, right. That's right. But only as of recently.'

'Well, not for the last, about, three months.'

'And now you're at that Italian place?'

'It's pan-European, not—'

'Ah, wow. And so, he's our age or something, this guy?'

'No, I think he's in his forties.'

'Oh, well, that's nothing. People in their forties are basically in their thirties, and people in their thirties are basically—'

'Actually, I'm pretty sure he's in his quite-late-forties.'

'And he's Italian?'

'No, he's from here.'

'And he owns the place?'

'Well, no. The executive chef and the investors *own* the restaurant, but, I mean, the head chef writes the menu and sources—'

Teddy nodded: 'All the fancy wines.'

'No, actually, we have a wine director who organises the wine list. Ellery sources the ingredients.'

'Oh-right-yeah. *Ellery*. Well, I love the dynamic; you're his right-hand woman in the kitchen, and then in the bedroom—'

'Well, actually, there's an assistant head chef called Nathan who's really more of his, like, deputy. I work below the two of them and oversee the—'

'But still, workplace romances are hot and exciting. And so, d'you think this is a one-time thing, or?'

'I hope not,' Julia said, thinking then about how often the things she thought she wanted turned out not to be the things she wanted. 'Are you ordering anything?'

It's a Date

A good and honest way to ask Ellery to do something the next night without revealing to him how fundamentally lonely of a person she was was to text him the following: 'Hey, I'm not seeing any of my friends tomo after work, so let me know if you maybe want to hang out?'

The Next Night, Ellery Postpones as They Leave the Restaurant

'I'm really sorry, but d'you mind if we maybe don't do this tonight?'

'No,' she said, 'of course not,' although she had spent almost her whole day thinking about it.

'I'm sorry, I have a thing I forgot about. My daughter needs me to—'

'Really, it's fine.'

'I'd still like to do this, though. Is tomorrow night doable?'

'Uh— Yes.'

'Are you sure?'

'Yep.'

'You're sure you're sure?'

Full-laugh: *You are making me laugh.* 'Yeah.'

Julia Gets an Answer

Ellery was wearing a reflective silver cycling jacket – which, in the dim evening light, Julia found particularly visually distracting – and also a deep-in-thought scowl. Julia's overlarge, light jacket billowed about her like a sail; her expression shifted intermittently between concerned and relaxed.

'I guess I mostly avoid alcohol as a way of avoiding other, worser substances,' Ellery was saying. 'Worse substances. Did avoid. Avoid-*ed*. But now it's been so long since anything bad happened, I can basically fully trust myself again.'

'So, for how long were you—?'

'Until last year I had used absolutely no substances for maybe – about four years? Is that right? Yeah, three or four. No opiates, no alcohol. My insubstantial years, is what I call them.'

'Funny.'

'It isn't easy to not do drugs or drink, working in hospitality and stuff. Basically it's an occupational hazard

53

– especially when you have my shitty back. But it's not so much that "doing" "drugs" or "drinking" "alcohol" was ever really my real problem anyway. The problem was more like, how I would use those substances as a crutch to basically excuse my not being my best self at work or with my kid or whatever – problems way deeper than any drug. Actually, maybe that isn't fully true, pills really were a problem for me; but I only ever quit drinking just to see if I could. And I think I have a much better handle on it nowadays, my drinking and behaving – I know I do. And also, if I ever did start acting like a total scumbag again, I know you'd be the first in line to tell me I'm fucking up. Julia.'

In the City

Because she'd seemed interested in it before, he took her to the upscale, overpriced restaurant in the city's financial district where he'd first learned to cook. Despite the intervening years, the elderly maître d' recognised Ellery on sight and treated him with great affection.

Dining with Ellery in the art-deco-style, time-worn restaurant made Julia feel half like his spoiled wife and half like his spoiled daughter. They sat, boothed, across from one another on facing maroon leather banquettes and ate a series of ornately presented dishes that Julia had expected – based on price alone (the entrée of crostini, dripping and speck cost about as much as Cascine's average main course) – would all taste far better than they actually did.

After the meal, Ellery requested the bill and looked, upon receiving it, horrified.

'Is everything okay?' Julia said, unsure of whether to offer to split the bill, which she probably couldn't afford, and from which, she presumed, no discount had been deducted.

'Yeah,' Ellery said, 'I just wasn't expecting – *this*.'

The Internet

'Be honest,' she said. 'Have you ever looked me up online?'

'On the internet?'

'Yeah.'

'Why?'

'I'm curious.'

'No, I mean, what reason would I have to look you up on the internet? I see you basically every day.'

'I don't know. To research. To look at pics.'

'In all honesty, no. But should I take that to mean that you've looked *me* up online?'

'No, I haven't,' she said, aspecting her face away from his. She prided herself on maintaining only one social media account, an old Facebook profile she sometimes checked in on her sister with, and which she had also, several times, used to look up Ellery – it was possible she'd admit to having done so, if there'd been any trace of him online for her to find.

'*Although*,' she added, moments later, and told him about the website where she'd partially read the review of the restaurant months before.

'Is that the one where they call me "steady-handed"?'

'Yes!'

'I hate that. It's so damning with faint praise. Better to be actively bad than a steady hand.'

'Actually, I think they said you have a light touch.'

Ellery looked crushed. 'That's so much worse,' he said.

The Dud

She had waited for a night when she knew Margot would be out late at a co-worker's leaving party to invite Ellery over to the apartment for the first time. The party was set to span several city-centre bar-and-grills in the lead-up to a club night that began at eleven, affording her an evening's free space to entertain in privacy without the worlds of live-in landlord and lover having to intersect. She still felt on edge about revealing her interior life to Ellery, but tolerably so, now she had the apartment to herself.

In advance of his arrival, she'd dragged the dining table from the corner to the middle of the living room; rotated

the placement of the sofa by ninety degrees to accommodate the repositioned dining table; hoovered the vacant
patch of floor where the sofa had been; washed her hair;
cleaned her sheets; and started cooking dinner. Everything
would be reset by the time Margot came home.

She was laying the table when Ellery buzzed the intercom from outside; she buzzed the intercom back from the
hallway to admit him into the building. She opened the
apartment's front door and kissed him when he appeared
there – greatly enjoying the novelty, never before having
greeted him this way.

'Come in,' she said, even though Ellery was already
inside by the time she said so. 'Throw your jacket in my
room.' She gestured at her bedroom door.

Ellery placed his arm against that door, said 'Big
moment,' and entered her room arm-first.

Julia stood in the hallway, staring ceilingward.

'In His service is perfect freedom,' Ellery read aloud
from a hoop-framed cross-stitch Julia's mother had
embroidered years ago. Julia didn't know why she still
toted the embroidery around with her from bedroom to
bedroom as an adult.

'C'mon,' she said, acting like she hadn't heard him,
'dinner's almost ready.

'Well, it's *almost* almost ready,' she added to herself,
back in the kitchenette.

'I like your little room,' Ellery said.

'Thanks,' Julia said. 'The kitchen's little too. Now, go sit at the little table.'

She fixed them both drinks and told Ellery someone would be right along to take his order, and he laughed.

As soon as Julia served their dinner, she started pointing out its flaws. The braised lamb neck had 'literally no flavour whatsoever', she complained, while chewing, 'I overdid it.' Also, the bitter-leaf side salad paired poorly with the main. 'I'm a fraud of a chef,' she said, finger-tracing nervous circles over the tabletop, 'a dud.'

Ellery was drinking fast and eating slowly; said he was enjoying his meal, 'And don't disparage my favourite chef like that.'

Julia said thank you, they touched hands, then the apartment door rattled – the moment felt supernatural.

Probably just a passage of air, Julia thought, maybe a neighbour had opened a window somewhere in the stairwell.

The door rattled again, but it wasn't until it rattled for a third time that Julia looked over and apprehended the noise's cause: Margot had returned home hours ahead of schedule.

'What's going on here?' Margot said, closing the door behind her and entering the living room; eyes scanning all the moved-around furniture. She looked at Ellery, then at Julia. 'I like what you've done with the place.'

Julia was too embarrassed by Margot's intrusion to register right-this-second just how embarrassed she was; she introduced her to Ellery and then vice versa, afterward making a quick joke about how they ate like this whenever Margot went out.

'Ve-ry in-ter-est-ing,' Margot said, perching on an arm of the displaced sofa. She proceeded to launch into a stream-of-consciousness, unasked-for account of the comedy of work-night-out-related errors that'd led to her getting ejected from a bar before overgrounding back home early enough to intrude on Julia's secret dinner.

After her story, Ellery – who had been smiling the whole time, but working too many muscles in his face to look like he was really relaxed – quizzed Margot about her job, which Margot replied she didn't even like, let alone want to talk about.

To Julia's dismay, Margot sloped off the arm and settled into the seat section of the sofa, leaning her head against its backrest in a way that suggested she intended to spend some time there.

'I couldn't possibly handle another drink,' Margot said, as if declining something she'd been offered. She added, 'So, where'd you two meet?' and Julia – staring at her and Ellery's cooling, half-finished meals – ascertainably annoyed, said, 'We work together, Margot.'

Only then realising the effect her interruption had had

on what was clearly a special night for Julia, Margot
exerted deliberate, downward effort into the sofa with
her elbows, slowly boosting herself up to a standing position. 'Well, you guys,' she said, pointing finger-guns at
the both of them, 'have a good rest-of-your-evening.'

Framed in the doorway as she departed the room, Margot turned around and, behind Ellery's back, gave Julia a
double thumbs-up; mouthed: *Good job*.

Julia Forgets How to Swallow

One evening out eating Thai, Julia accidentally
second-guessed the act of glottal faith essential to the exe-
cution of a swallow; the trust-fall of food from pharynx to
oesophagus, a bodily function which – like blinking, urinating or falling asleep – was easier to accomplish without
being too aware of it.

As her mouthful of tamarind-glazed duck and jasmine
rice verged on the precipice of her soft palate, she felt the
onset of paralysis in the muscles of her throat; her automatic swallowing mechanism halting and windpipe fully
obstructed – a waking apnoea. She wondered whether she
might die right here at this Thai place, and if she died,
would Ellery and her mother have to meet.

Moving deliberately and without breathing, she reached
both hands across the table toward a luxury-brand bottle

of mineral water, distributed a long pour into an empty glass, and raised that glass carefully to her lips. With the water's weight and pressure, she compelled her body into forcibly swallowing the food.

The relief of being able to in- and exhale like normal again made her almost fully cry. She blinked back a few subtle tears and did not mention what'd happened to Ellery, who himself hadn't noticed anything untoward. The meal, he later told her, had not been to his liking.

Ellery in Pain

In his bathroom at a weird hour of the night, Ellery was wincing while topically applying a palmful of prescription-strength liniment cream onto his lower back – around that same area, he'd also adhered an octagon of kinesiology tape like an occult symbol.

Julia entered the bathroom and said hey, could she help. Ellery said no because the pain was in the base of his spine and then when Julia tried to massage there he said no, she hadn't listened – the pain wasn't *at* the base of his spine but *in* it, where no one could reach. He apologised for snapping at her and, honey, she said, honey don't worry.

Another Question

On his fire-exit balcony, in the middle of a conversation about something else, she asked him: 'What makes you happy?'

The question had just slipped out and she regretted it immediately – it sounded girlish and not like anything a person Ellery's own age would've asked.

She thought about saying 'The restaurant, right?' to disburden him of the need to answer, but when she looked over, he appeared to be seriously weighing the question.

The evening air was cold and smelled of man-made substances being burned. She took another sip of natural wine and watched the downtown lights.

Ellery stayed quiet for so long she felt sure he was going to retort with something lofty and drunk, like, 'What even *is* happiness, anyway?' But his reply was disarming, sincere: 'Being around you.'

Weekends

On Mondays and Tuesdays, which were her weekends, she hovered around the apartment while Margot was at work, making the most of the space.

With the living room to herself, she might light some incense, maybe masturbate around – sometimes loiter in Margot's room and rummage through her personal belongings: flip through the businessy-looking self-help books stacked across her modular shelving system that had words like 'mindset' or 'trick' in their titles; observe, on Margot's walls, the decade-and-a-half-old, low-megapixel digital photo-printouts depicting her with Julia's sister at various festivals and parties, both a lot worse-dressed but happier-looking back then.

Or, if she'd stayed the night at Ellery's, she'd occupy herself with Ellery-versions of those same timepass, privacy-breaching activities – maybe also AeroPress some coffee, try to work his entertainment centre. She always made sure to feel guilty when she searched for any opiates or high-concentration painkillers he'd stashed around his apartment, but also always allowed for her guilt to be surpassed by relief when, inevitably, she found none.

More of the Same

They had eaten a multicourse meal at a restaurant occupying the renovated mezzanine deck of a Sackler-funded contemporary arts space.

Walking home, he said he was still hungry, and when they got back to his apartment, she baked two peaches and watched as he ate them both with ice cream. He was maybe the most unselfconscious eater she had ever seen, perhaps also the greediest.

'I know, I'm a pig,' he said, correctly guessing her thought. 'And the worst part is, I don't even care what I'm eating. It's like, I just want to eat a bunch of *something*. I just want to dive in. I'd eat a stack of unbuttered toast, so long as there was enough of it.'

'I don't mind,' she said, standing over him while he ate. There was an animal loose inside of him, and it was always hungry. 'I think it's nice you have a big appetite.'

'Well, in that case,' he said, raising his empty bowl toward her, 'could you maybe see if there's any more of those peaches?'

Irregardless

They were walking over salt over ice in the park; she was hugging his right arm with both of her arms.

They were joke-arguing about the word 'irregardless'; Ellery said it didn't exist, while Julia maintained that it did.

After she'd consulted her smartphone and won the argument, Julia spotted Owen, looking down at his own smartphone, agog, walking toward them in the opposite direction. Out of sheer surprise, she slowed down and called out his name. She was only half-aware of Ellery wresting his arm free from her embrace.

Owen looked around, resituating himself, then beelined

over to greet them. 'I thought that sounded like you,' he said to Julia, 'but then I was like, no, wait. Is that her?'

'And then it was me,' Julia said.

'Correct,' Owen said, bouncing on the balls of his feet to keep warm. 'So, what's up with you guys?'

'Not much,' Ellery said, 'just walking. Maybe getting some lunch.'

'Together?' Owen said, eyebrows arching slightly.

'Oh, no,' Ellery said. 'Well, I mean, yeah. Just as a lunch thing.'

Julia stretched her hands out by her sides then slipped them into the front pocket of Ellery's hoodie, which she was wearing.

They all stood conferring for a while longer, and after they'd gotten to their conversation's first silence, Owen referenced having somewhere to be, said goodbye, and left.

She definitely wasn't sulking, but, as they resumed their walk, Julia intentionally refrained from initiating conversation.

Without ever really having discussed it, they'd kept up a certain distance around one another at the restaurant – a tactful partition between work life and love life that, to Julia, seemed cultured and refined. But seeing Ellery use that distance to, well, distance himself from her made the whole thing feel cheapened, degraded.

He extended a hand into the air then closed it around nothing. 'Sorry,' he said, eventually. 'I just thought it'd make life easier. For now. To not mention about—'

'Completely understood,' she said, although she wasn't so sure she did understand. Still, she managed to push aside all her previous thoughts and not get too frowny. Before they discussed anything else, she added: 'You do not need to explain our relationship to me.'

Stephanie Says Nothing

The next morning – before anyone else had yet arrived – Stephanie cornered Julia in the kitchen and said: 'So, you and Ellery?'

Feeling the sides of her face variegating to red, Julia said, 'Me and Ellery what?'

'How long've you two been—?'

'Oh, no. We're just friends. We sometimes go out for drinks but—'

'Uh-huh,' Stephanie said, smiling annoyingly as she opened the dishwasher and started transferring its contents into a plastic carrying tray.

'No, seriously,' Julia insisted, feeling a sudden sense of obligation to maintain her aforesaid lie, 'really nothing's going on. You should come out with us next time.'

Stephanie looked up at Julia from her bent-over position

66

holding a handful of clean utensils and did a more annoying version of the same smile as before. 'Uh-huh.'

'Okay,' Julia said, circling her hand at the wrist a few times, 'we are seeing each other, kind of. But it's only recent and not very serious.' She felt surprised to feel so disappointed that the clandestine phase of their relationship – which she'd expected to last for a few more weeks – had already concluded.

At that moment, Ellery rode into view of the kitchen's single casement window, sideways-dismounting his bicycle while it was still in motion.

'Don't worry,' Stephanie said. 'Who would I even tell?'

Guest Espresso

Ellery, who apparently knew and was known by name to the staff of Julia's go-to coffee place, ordered a flat white for her and a guest espresso for himself. The head barista – whom Julia felt the need to make clear to Ellery she also knew, in her own no-name way – dismissed her attempt at payment after returning her greeting.

'How is it that you know everyone?' Julia said, affixing a plastic lid to her coffee cup, which took three tries to properly secure.

'Well,' Ellery said, outside now. He itched along his hairline and adopted the mockingly didactic rule-voice

Julia had never outwardly objected to him using: 'I guess I'm just an incredibly popular person.'

Can I Tell You Something I'm Ashamed Of?

'Uh-huh sure,' she said.

It was after closing, just her and Nathan in the kitchen. She was in the process of pre-poaching five dozen eggs for tomorrow's brunch.

'It isn't a big thing,' Nathan said.

'So what is it?' With her back to him, she continued cracking eggs into a stainless-steel mixing bowl. 'I'm listening.'

'Actually no,' he said. 'It doesn't matter.'

'No, no, I'm listening.'

'Yeah, no,' he said. 'Doesn't matter.'

She turned around to face him, an empty half-eggshell in each hand. She hadn't thought she was in a bad mood tonight, but maybe she was. 'Jesus, Nathan. Either say what you want to say or grow up. Just don't act like *this*. It's childish.'

Lovers

They were eating skewers of freshwater unagi in a cubical room that had, two months prior, domiciled a functioning laundrette.

68

'I can name all mine by heart.'

Across from her, he stirred in his seat. 'Is that right?'

She took a drink of her drink. 'By heart and in chronological order.'

Being tired, he surrendered to having the conversation she wanted them to have. 'Go ahead.'

She counted them out on her fingers as she recited each of their names, starting over anew on her right hand after she'd gotten to Anthony. 'David, Aaron, Matt G., Joel, Ezra, Shane, Josh, Daniel, Luke, Anthony, Nick, Tom, Chris, Matt C., Alex.'

'So not a whole—'

She raised her left hand, a fist with the thumb extended: 'Plus you.' She felt embarrassed, and remembered remembering from suchlike occasions in the past that her life was always out to embarrass her. She had acted recklessly, and Ellery now had nothing to say. She tapped the white tabletop between them. 'I won't ask you for yours.'

Saturday Market

At Ellery's insistence, they'd taken an early shift off to meet his daughter at the Saturday street market where she sold her handmade whiteware ceramics. The market was often listed in listicles of weekend events to attend

69

in the city and was therefore densely crowded; as they walked, they passed through the frames of multiple smart-phone-captured photos and video recordings.

The mostly cashless artisanal stalls sold gourmet street food; minimalist floral arrangements; upcycled furniture; fair-trade baked goods; boutique jewellery; ethical shapewear; alternative milks; 3D-printed cutlery; vintage spectacles; fretwork-design greeting cards, etc.

Julia felt it necessary to somehow engage with each of the stalls as she moved past them; to at least smile at their owners, who mostly smiled back at her. Ellery seemed distracted, walking slowly, and when she asked him if everything was okay he said something about his sciatica then affirmed that everything was golden.

Julia noticed a lot of little kids toddling around; a lot of littler kids being carried in Björns or prams. Embarrassing to admit that the thought of Ellery nurturing a tiny dependant was the fantasy image of him that recurred to her most frequently; strange now to be meeting his young-adult daughter.

'Where'd she say to find her?'

'She should be—' he said, scanning the stalls as they walked. 'She should be right—' Unsure from a distance then surer the closer they got, Julia realised they were steadily approaching a young woman whose facial contours were directly mappable onto Ellery's; blur your eyes slightly and the resemblance became clearer.

Ellery made introductions and they all hugged over the counter of his daughter's stall; the displayed ceramics clattering between them.

'Hey, nice coat,' Ellery said. 'I used to have one just like it.'

'Sadly for you it looks better on me.'

'I fondly remember a time when you used to make fun of how I dressed.'

Julia noted the substantial weight differential between herself and Ellery's daughter with some pleasure, then noted guilt at having noted that pleasure. 'These plates are so amazing.'

'Oh, thanks.'

'I'm, like, really amazed. It's really—'

'It's nice to finally meet you. Dad's been telling me a lot about—'

'Same, it's really—'

'—how talented you are.'

'Not true. I only ever tell her how average you are.'

'He's showing off. You know he thinks you're—'

'These plates just look so— I can't believe how amazing these plates look.' Julia stared deliberately hard at the plates to convey her disbelief.

'Yeah, I'm always trying to get your boyfriend to, like, buy a stack of them for his fake Italian restaurant.'

'Well, firstly: it isn't my restaurant. Secondly: it isn't Italian at all, real or fake.'

'I've been saying forever they need to change the name.'

'And thirdly: tableware isn't even my responsibility.'

'What's going on with you, anyway? How's your back? You were walking like an old person over there.'

'Was I? Normally it's fine, but it has been kind of bad today. It's because of the surfaces at work; I have to stoop down to use them.'

'Were you working this morning already?'

'No, but—'

'I think all the cycling he does is worse than—'

'Have you been going to your Pilates classes?'

A miniature dog, bred eugenically to exaggerate the cutest qualities of its pedigree, circled Julia's feet. The dog breathed like it couldn't breathe.

'Is this yours?'

'I go to the classes when I have the time.'

'Yeah.'

'But it's rare that I actually have the time.'

'So *cute*.' The dog forced its head between Julia's ankles; she knelt and petted it lightly. 'What's its name?'

'I call him Kitten, but honestly, I don't think he even gets that he *has* a name.'

'Hi Kitten, hi Kitten.'

Ellery crouched and petted the dog alongside Julia;

the dog rolled over and yapped as he administered some robust scratches to its stomach. If Ellery were a dog, Julia thought, he'd be a German shepherd or a golden retriever; a dumb dog everybody liked with a big dick.

Ellery, addressing Julia but directing his baby-talk tone toward the dog: 'Just call him whatever you like. This guy's as dumb as rocks.'

'Dad, please stop scratching Kitten so hard.'

'Why?' Ellery said. He scratched the dog with both hands; the dog rolled around in ecstasy and wagged its tail. 'See. He likes it.'

Leaving the Market

Above, a drifting bank of clouds lent further shade to the spring noon's dusk-like dark; Ellery prompted a round of goodbyes by mentioning the possibility of rain. Before they left, Julia purchased two plates from Ellery's daughter – a purchase they transacted contactlessly.

Despite being much younger than Julia, Ellery's daughter seemed far more mature and put-together than she was: her dog; her stall; her trade. Being around her, Julia was reminded of girls she'd attended high school with who'd stayed in their hometown after graduating, accelerating prematurely through major life milestones into stages of adulthood well beyond their years. Thinking about those girls made Julia feel sad and so, purposely, she thought of other things.

It Kills

Julia had been taking a combined oral contraceptive for some time before they jointly decided Ellery should stop wearing condoms; the dual birth controls overlapping by a few weeks in terms of usage but not necessarily, she knew, protective efficacy.

Two mornings after the first time Ellery came inside her she awoke early with the feeling of a deep contusion in her pelvis; pain severe enough for her to involuntarily picture the affected area as a glowing bullseye irradiated by thermal- or night-vision-coloured light – a mental image she'd assimilated from years of exposure to advertisements for over-the-counter analgesics.

If she moved slowly and breathed shallowly enough she could almost manage not to feel the pain – let it settle and diffuse to an undetectable level – but expending bodily energy in any direction brought it coalescing back to her centre.

She toughed things out all the way to work until, in the staff bathroom, she urinated what felt like one long, serrated knife-edge. Afterward, she got up too quickly and had to stand there while static cleared from her vision like she was waiting for a car windshield to demist. The pain had turned heavy and triangular-shaped, and she couldn't stop needing to pee.

In the kitchen, taking great effort to at once conceal the pain and also conceal the level of effort it took for her to conceal the pain, she inhaled a deep, sore breath and announced to Ellery and Owen: 'Hey guys, I don't mean to sound dramatic here, but I think I should maybe go to the doctor's.'

Ellery, concerned: 'Are you okay?'

'Yeah, no, I'm fine. It's just—' She knew she would feel embarrassed later for having uttered this phrase in earshot of Owen: 'It's girl stuff. Will you be—?'

'Owen and I'll survive.' Ellery slid a tray of duck-fat-glazed vegetables into the oven. 'Do you need—?'

'It's fine, it's fine.' She untied her apron, blinking hot tears down into the pits of her eyes. She took another painful breath, steeled herself, and added, 'It's fine.'

The UTI

After she'd inputted her personal information and the details of her symptoms into a touchscreen monitor and the system that monitor was networked to had processed those data, Julia walked into the walk-in clinic's waiting room.

The tandem chairs all faced the same way, like

75

auditorium seating; Julia selected one that allowed for a buffer space between her and the nearest sick person on either side.

On her smartphone, she read several Mumsnet threads documenting other women's accounts of having suffered through UTIs; in another tab she opened a glossary of common-usage Mumsnet acronyms. She remembered having two or maybe three UTIs when she'd been younger, and was pretty sure that neither or none of them had been as bad as this one.

She received a text from Ellery: 'hows it going x'

She replied: 'Sent from the kitchen?'

'no haha from the office.' He appended: 'did you get a docs appt?'

Using her smartphone while being this ill made Julia feel sort of motion sick, but it was nice to contend with a source of irritation located outside of her body. 'Yeah.'

'good. owens worried.'

'Tell him dont be!'

'but everything ok?'

She made a loose fist with her unoccupied hand and tapped it against her cheek. 'Yeah.'

Nathan vs Antibiotics

The overprescription of antibiotics causes common viruses to evolve into antimicrobially resistant, hypervirulent strains, Nathan told her later that week. And the use of antibiotics in the production of commercial beef poses a potentially catastrophic threat to human health.

If He Looks at Me in the Next Five Seconds, Tonight I Will Tell Him I Love Him

Drunk at a matinée hour in the heatless early-April sun and surrounded by good friends – or whatever tier of friendship one classifies close colleagues as – they were all seated around two dragged-together tables in the beer garden behind a community pub.

The group's males were drinking pints of the same cask-conditioned ale from nonic glasses; Julia and Stephanie drank G&Ts served in highballs each containing a couple of red-and-white-striped paper straws.

Julia returned from the bar with a fresh round of drinks and, after distributing them, tried to retake her former corner seat next to Ellery, which he'd slid into and claimed for himself. 'Scooch over,' she said, and Ellery replied, in a pacific monotone, 'Make me.' In play-antagonism she sat on his lap, then, sensing tension in his legs, moved further down the bench to sit beside Owen.

Stephanie said: 'Has anyone heard from Lena recently?'

'I haven't,' Ellery said.

Nathan exhaled, 'I know she's in Berlin,' a cloud of menthol-infused mist whiting out his face; he'd recently transitioned from smoking cigarettes to smoking cartridges of glycerine-based, nicotine-salt-containing syrup from a vaporiser identical in shape and weight to a standard USB flash drive. 'And she works at some vegan place. And she has a cat.'

'Truly insane you know all that considering she and I were proper friends and she literally hasn't answered a text from me in weeks.'

'Yeah, well, let's just say I keep a watchful eye on old Lena using a little resource I like to call: the worldwide web.'

While everyone else continued talking around her, Julia stared ahead at a shrub drunkenly enough and for long enough to experience a slight zooming-in and sideward-panning of her vision – a Ken Burns effect – vaguely dissociating from then gradually reassociating back into her body; the realisation dawning on her that soon she would need to head home, or to Ellery's home. The day had revealed the fullness of its dimensions and she was satisfied, tired and contented in the blue light of the late afternoon. She swerved a look uptable toward Ellery – tried and failed to catch his eye.

If he looks at me in the next five seconds, tonight I will tell him I love him. One, two, three, four.

A Code for the Bathroom

The next morning, Julia arrived late to work and became quickly aware, once she'd started her shift, of having intruded into a post-argument environment; long-held silence reverberating as an active acoustic presence in the kitchen.

'Is everything okay with you boys?' she asked, after a half-hour of being caught crossways between Ellery and Nathan's mutual, non-verbal frigidity.

'Completely golden.'

Rather than trying to infer anything from Ellery's reply, Julia attempted to make Nathan laugh. 'Nathan, remember when that guy shouted at you because you wouldn't give him a code for the bathroom? And you were like: *There is no code for the bathroom!* And he didn't believe you?'

Nathan nodded half-heartedly and continued ribboning root vegetables.

'Ay-yai-yai,' Julia said, resigning herself to tiptoeing around whatever unspoken thing was going on between the men for the rest of the day.

At lunch, when Nathan headed outside for a vape break, Julia asked Ellery what was going on.

'I don't think you'd understand.'

'Yeah, well,' she said, realising she had nothing else really to say, 'maybe I would.'

Fusion

After their shift, Julia convinced Ellery to take her to the soft launch of a much-hyped but in reality only-okay African-fusion eatery where they sat on tatami cushions and ate six-bite concept dishes which, she remarked, each seemed only to contain about three bites'-worth of actual flavour. 'And also' – she gestured at the overhead fixture – 'the lighting here is *horrific*.'

Seeking a backrest against which to lean, Ellery reclined on his cushion by several degrees, then, losing his balance, recalled the design of the seat he had sat upon, quickly tipping himself forward again to swallow the mouthful of food he was chewing, and to finish his drink.

When next he spoke, he addressed the air about an inch to the left of Julia's face, managing to stop himself short of saying anything worse than: 'Do you think, maybe, when we go out somewhere expensive to eat, you could do something other than, like, tell me how many guys you've fucked or just sit and complain the whole time?'

Caloric Deficit

Like most chefs, Julia at home subsisted on a low-quality diet of comfort foods and quick meals, almost all of which she ate standing up in the kitchenette with accompanying feelings of shame. Rarely these days, unless she and Ellery went out somewhere, did she eat what you or her mother might call an 'actual dinner'.

Quality Control

Mid-service, Ellery asked if he could taste the dish Julia had just prepared and she said sure. Rather than simply breaking off a sliver of the buttermilk-fried pork medallion with a sidelong tine of his fork the way he might usually sample her work, he impaled and raised the entire six-ounce slab of meat to his mouth from its serving plate – an action which, at first, Julia thought was a joke.

As he champed down hard on the pork his expression changed, then changed into several other expressions after that. He replaced the remaining bitten portion back onto its plate, then spat alongside it a disfigured bolus of chewed meat, at which Julia directed her gaze.

'Really bad. Not good.'

'Why,' she said. 'What's wrong with it?'

'You just need to do it over.'

'Well, elaborate please, so I don't make the same mistake again.'

'Just do it over,' he said. 'It's substandard. I'm not trying to start a—'

'Fine, fine,' she said, adding, in enraged compliance, 'yes, Chef.'

'Are you—?'

'Maybe just go away for now.'

'Okay. I'll do that.'

For several seconds Julia stared at the floor, wondering whether she should try to continue feeling normal or if she should let herself get upset. Not having heard any footsteps receding away from her, she presumed that, if she turned around, she would find Ellery still standing over her shoulder. When she abruptly about-faced to tell him to really just leave her alone, she was surprised to find him already gone.

How We Fail Others and Also Ourselves

Due, she sometimes liked to imagine, to an interesting and traumatic event buried somewhere in her past that she'd never as yet been able to locate but would someday discover and then overcome in an entertaining and highly retellable way, Julia had not yet learned to participate in face-to-face arguments as anything other than an alkalising force.

It was while privately attempting to guess at exactly what her specific repressed trauma might be – on another night after they'd left another restaurant, with Ellery having aired another new grievance related to her behaviour – that she found herself unaccountably on the verge of tears and making blanket apologies for being the way she was; trying to explain to him that it was hard for her, when he acted mean, to articulate exactly how she felt in real time, hard for her to break the lifelong habit of saving up her feelings until she could be alone with them.

'And I do try. To be communicative. I do try *so hard* to be communicative.' Only in hearing herself repeating this phrase did Julia realise how drunk she was.

'It's okay. I didn't mean to be so—' Ellery's hand opened gently against the small of her back.

At skyline level, the overfull moon shone overly brightly, as if illuminated from the inside. Julia asked whether there was anything astrologically weird going on that night and Ellery said he didn't know. She took a picture of the moon with her smartphone but it came out small and normal-looking onscreen. He said, 'You'll just have to remember it weird.'

By the time they got home, the atmosphere between them was almost fully restored; they really did love each other and, lying on top of Ellery's bed while listening to him brushing his teeth as she undid her jeans, Julia remembered all the good times they'd had together – she thought again of the size of the moon.

Ellery came in and turned out the big light, and the room seemed instantly colder.

Free Association

The object of the game, she explained, was for both players to say the first word they thought of at the same time. The game would continue until they both said the same thing simultaneously. She asked if he was ready to play and he said yes.

'Plate,' she said, signalling for him to talk.

A moment later he said, 'Hello.'

'Okay,' she said. 'That was just a test.'

He said nothing, thinking of what to say next.

'Chef,' she said. 'Walk,' he said, at the same time.

'Out.'	'Empty.'
'Face.'	'Eclipse.'

'Eclip—' she said. Then, 'Wow, no.'

'Pill,' he had said.

'Trick.'	'Hands.'
'Day.'	'Feet.'
'Sun.'	'Shoe.'
'Cushion.'	'Sky.'
'Eat.'	'Away.'

'Night.'	'Cheat.'
'Date.'	'Walk.'
'Fade.'	'Uh—'
'Fate.'	'Wall.'
'Talk.'	'Globe.'
'Mother.'	'Grass.'
'Table.'	'Window.'
'Home.'	'Home.'

The Almoner

One midnight, leaving the restaurant alone, Julia passed three laughing homeless women, each one prettier and younger-looking than herself, sitting upright in their sleeping bags against the concrete steps that led to the newly refurbished town hall, a building she had only ever seen open to accommodate weddings.

Feeling collaterally responsible for the women's lives of hardship due to Cascine's and her own upwardly mobile, rent-inflating presences in the late-stage-regeneration neighbourhood, she headed back to the restaurant and reopened its kitchen to cook, in the dark and with tears in her eyes, three from-scratch, nutritive risotto-based dinners.

Only when she'd returned and already delivered the meals to the women did she read the outdoor-proof

PVC banner leaning aslant against the stair above them: *Sponsored sleep-out. Raising money and awareness for homelessness in our community.*

'This is so kind,' the middle and most facially symmetrical of the three young women said, inhaling rising steam from an open Tupperware. 'You're literally an angel.'

The Future

In the park, beneath clouds so wide and horizontal they looked like they were being displayed in the wrong aspect ratio, they sat drinking coffee on a memorial bench.

Ellery was explaining to Julia the management's long-term plan for Cascine, which involved expanding the restaurant's dining area to seat an extra twelve-ish covers that could be served without the need for hiring any additional kitchen- or waitstaff, thereby achieving an economy of scale.

Julia felt like she didn't have enough personal meaning attached to the idea to really get invested in it, but it was nice to sit and listen to Ellery talk with such enthusiasm; nice to hear his optimistic thoughts about how the future would go.

'And then, what do you think'll happen after that?' she said, swirling her coffee cup in circles as if to replenish its contents from the remaining dregs.

'The restaurant'll make more money.'

'And then?'

'We'll all be happier.'

'And then?'

He absently ran his palms along the lengths of his thighs. 'After that, I don't know.'

Ellery's Attachment Style

'I worry that my partner cares less about me than I care about them.'

'Say my options again?'

'Strongly agree, somewhat agree, neither agree nor disagree, somewhat disagree, strongly disagree.'

'You definitely think I'm going to say strongly disagree.'

'I just ask the questions.'

'Neither agree nor disagree.'

She rolled her eyes in a way he couldn't not-notice and selected the middle of the five selectable radio buttons. Funny how it was impossible to return to the state of never having selected any button after you'd selected one of them. You could select a different button and switch your answer, but could not go back to the lifetime of pure potential you'd spent never having submitted to the limited logic of selecting an option from the questionnaire's scale of multiple choices.

'Okay, next: I do whatever my partner wants or tells me to do.'

He thought. 'Say the options for me one more time?'

'Strongly agree, somewhat agree, neither agree nor disagree, somewhat disagree, strongly disagree.'

'Somewhat agree.' The air between them seemed altered. He looked at her. 'What?'

'*I do whatever my partner wants or tells me to do.* Is the question.'

'I heard it the first time, and I somewhat agree with it.'

'Okay,' she said, and selected the button correspondent to Ellery's answer. She wondered whether she should say the thing she was thinking.

'And it isn't a question,' he said. 'It's a statement.'

The Message

Did you know about this: that to safeguard your privacy and security, instant messages sent to you from non-friends via Facebook's dedicated chat platform are filtered through to an inbox subfolder entitled 'Message Requests'? And that you don't receive any badge or push notifications when these unsolicited messages get delivered to you, because most of them are sent by bots?

Julia was up late, anticipating a scheduled Facebook Messenger exchange with her sister, who was living eight hours into the future, Indochina Time. She was absorbing information from multiple sources simultaneously: reading a long-read while looking at items of clothing and imagining herself wearing them.

More out of boredom than actual curiosity, she opened then touchpadded away from her Messenger account's default 'Recent' inbox (navigating past her sister's name and the grey dot beside it indicating that she was offline), toward her Message Requests subfolder.

Upon opening her Message Requests subfolder – something she hadn't done in over a year – Julia discovered a queue of three unread chats there waiting for her. Two were from fake-looking accounts sharing offer codes for discount Ray-Bans, and the third was from Lena.

The entire log of messages she'd received from Lena was about five inches long on her laptop's display, spanning four discrete grey, round-cornered text boxes. The individual timestamps next to each message revealed that they'd been sent within a five-minute period between 02:21 and 02:26 on a Friday morning two months earlier.

'Greetings chef!' read the first message. The second read: 'I hop this messeag', the third: 'Ooops', and the fourth: 'I hope this message finds you well. I am writing to ask you to tell your junky stalker boyf to stop fucking messaging me and calling me and to leave me the fuck alone. I have blocked him everywhere I can and still he doesn't take thethe fucking hint I am asking you to tell him I am not interested in him and his bullshit life and if you have any sense you will get out of there as soon as you can. Julia I didn't realise at the time but he is a psycho. You seem good and I was sorry to hear you got roped in by his fucked bullshit. If you have been waiting for a red flag this is the red flag you have been waiting for.'

Julia stared at the message for so long that when she finally looked away from it, she kept seeing its afterimage superimposed over her immediate surroundings.

She was having trouble disbelieving what she had read. She thought about Ellery and Lena for a long time. She thought about Ellery taking serial interest in his younger, female employees. She wondered where Lena was now. And after she'd spent several hours back-and-forthing over thoughts like these by herself in the dark, she decided she simply had not read the message.

Julia Gets Awakened by a Call

'Tell me everything about this guy you're seeing or else I'll tell Ma what little I already know.'

'Hey, what?'

'Are you awake?'

'No. I mean, you woke me up. But I don't know what "guy" you're referring to.'

'The same "guy" Marg says she's thinking of starting charging for rent.'

'She what? He's literally only stayed here, like, three times.'

'It actually worked! I *knew* you were seeing someone!'

'Oh.'

'I could tell! And I was right!'

'Oh, you old slyboots.'

'Even when I'm halfway around the world I can always tell. I can always *feel* it.'

'You tricked me.'

'So, what's his name?'

'Please, no. It's just a very casual arrangement.'

'Mmmm, staying over three times doesn't exactly sound like my idea of a *very*—'

'Now's really honestly not the greatest moment to be getting into it. Did Margot tell you about this?'

'No, I genuinely just had a hunch. I followed all the available, y'know, *clues*. Such as: where were you last night? I was waiting on the internet.'

'I'm sorry. I was really tired.'

'Yeah, well, we're all tired. And you're in bed now?'

'I am.'

'What a slob.'

'Where's your husband-to-be?'

'Hiking. With a Sherpa. They make you go with a

Sherpa here. Apparently last month some guy got lost in the woods without a Sherpa and it took them, like, two weeks to find him. Because he'd *died*.'

'Jesus.'

'Yeah. Of starvation.'

'What time is it?'

'Or maybe exposure. But sometimes even the Sherpas die out here too, so I've heard. It's, I don't know. After-noon time.'

'It's six in the morning here. God.'

'Well, this is what you get when you sleep through a carefully scheduled Messenger date, Jewel; you get an annoyingly timed make-up-call. So, what celebrity docs your new boyfriend most look like?'

'Please don't.'

'Alright-okay-okay, we don't have to talk about it. But are you missing me?'

I Am Not Living the Right Life

Inevitably, her odds of thinking about Lena's message scaled in direct proportion to the intensity of her attempts to not think about it. Thoughts of the message became the involuntary afterthoughts that trailed behind every fore-thought of Ellery.

Unlike other intrusive thoughts she'd withstood in

92

the past that were easy to drown out with distraction or pave over with light activity, memories of Lena's message continued to endure despite weeks of concerted, multi-method shunning.

Occasionally – only making things worse – Julia circled around Lena's Facebook profile, where it looked like she was indeed living in Berlin and had reached her haircut's depressing grow-out stage. Should she reply to her? What would she even say?

Several times, at a meal or in bed or at work, she'd considered raising the issue with Ellery. Once, on her break, she'd spent an entire half-hour – forcing it slightly – crying in Cascine's cramped, antechamber-like office, where Ellery usually stored his bike and Nathan applied his extra mid-shift coat of deodorant, waiting for somebody to discover her there and ask, gently, what was wrong. But nobody had discovered her, nobody had gone looking. Probably she had hidden herself too well.

The Lure

The restaurant contained five souls, all employees. Ellery, Nathan and Julia were in the kitchen preparing for the coming lunch service, while – in the bar area – a newish waitstaff hire was training another, newer, waitstaff hire to operate the till's point-of-sale software.

From a sheathed position in its storage block, Julia withdrew a wide-bladed santoku knife, last professionally whetted several weeks prior – duller than she'd prefer, but still usable for the task of dividing a defrosting veal rib into separate chops. Julia laid her hand along the blade's spine to exert additional downward pressure over its cutting edge into the hardened meat. Unable to withstand the level of force she was applying, the blade began to tilt as she bore down upon it; the knife skewed to one side before giving way completely, its hilt slipping out of her grip and skittering across the worktop toward Nathan.

'Jesus,' Julia said. 'It's basically blunt.'

'Call the sharpener guy,' Nathan said. 'He's overdue.'

'Don't call him,' Ellery said, 'he's coming next month. The knives are fine. Julia, you just need to go easier on them. It's all about technique.'

'Right.'

'And frankly,' Ellery continued, 'if you'd left the rib to thaw for longer—'

'You always defend the thing, not me.'

'What?'

'Every time I have a problem with a thing, it's like you always automatically defend the object or the institution or the rule, whatever it is. You never take my side.'

'Why would I take your side if I knew you were wrong about something?'

'Because, it's not just about being right. You, like, relish the moments where you get to boss me around or teach me a lesson.'

'That's weird. So you're saying I behave like I'm your boss?'

'I know that this is all very funny to you, but honestly, yes, that is how I feel; outside of work especially. It's like you don't even like me, the way you treat me lately.'

'She has a point.'

'Nathan, please—'

'Just tell me,' Julia said, pausing for Nathan to exit the kitchen before continuing. 'Do you even like me anymore?'

'Name one example of this happening, this thing about me defending a thing.'

'Just now,' Julia said, eyes saccading toward the knife then back to Ellery.

'Name one other, actual example.'

'Do you, or do you not, like me anymore?'

'If the whole foundation of this argument you're trying to make us have is predicated on a claim you can't even back up—'

'Ellery, that's not the question.' She wasn't really yelling, but her voice had begun to climb into the lower registers of the yelling scale. She checked over her shoulder to see if the waitstaff were listening – which they were

– prompting them to look busy with their sidework.

'Name any other time this has happened.'

'Last week,' Julia said, not as a real response but to have at least said something.

'Last week?' Ellery said. 'What happened last week?'

A noise from the kitchen's wall-mounted Food Standards Agency guideline-compliant electrified insecticidal grid reported the termination of an adult housefly, lured in by the steady glow of the appliance's ultraviolet tube lights.

Julia said she didn't know.

Serenity Prayer

Nights later, after dark, Julia was alone, mopping the kitchen floor – something Owen had said he'd done but evidently hadn't. She was thinking extra-hard about what she was doing so she didn't have to think about how she was feeling.

Suds of diluted floorcare product dissolved under the soles of her Crocs. She turned around to examine the Croc-shaped discoloured footprints she'd tracked over a still-drying section of the floor. She mopped away those footprints then strode across the room to mop in a different area of the kitchen – treading, as she moved toward the uncleanly floorspace, yet more footprints over another section of the floor she'd already cleaned.

96

The problem with her technique was that she mopped in circles – standing in the centre of an unclean section and mopping all the reachable surrounding floor within the mop's handle-length radius. It occurred to her that to obtain optimal floor coverage and to keep from stepping into any previously cleaned areas, a professional custodian would probably mop the floor in stripes – walking backwards as they wiped their mop out in front of them, erasing all trace of themselves as they went.

The secret to effective mop-drying is to get a twist in the mophead's strands of saturated cloth before impressing them into the bucket's built-in wringer. Both apparatuses in the value-brand mop-and-bucket set Julia was using had the word 'Turbo' printed down their sides. At her old work, they'd used a modern, name-brand mop you'd had to load with separately purchasable microfibre cloths and that'd had a sprayer mechanism built into its handle.

After drying it possibly too hard, she submerged the mophead into the rinse-water that had turned an opaque slate-grey. When she stirred the unexpectedly weight-less-feeling mop in a looping figure-eight motion to absorb into it a maximal amount of water, she realised – from the lightness of its handle – that the mop's non-detachable head must've broken off inside the bucket.

Only to confirm to herself this thing that she basically already knew did she poke around underwater with the submerged end of the handle to feel for the sunken mop-head – which she hit upon immediately – before raising the handle's now nubbed, wetted tip above the liquid's darkened surface.

To retrieve the mophead she would have to immerse her hand into the bucket's stagnant grey water and kitchen-floor debris. At the thought of doing so, she javelinned the mop handle onto the floor, the speed and violence of which action, afterward, made her feel deranged.

Looking down at the bucket with the handle lying alongside it, her body seemed suddenly to itch all over; she hated the way her clothes were touching her. She wanted to scream forever and never make another noise in her life both at once. She tried to say the Serenity Prayer but was overcome by frustration and rage; sobs wracked her body like dry heaves. 'Oh, fuck you fuck you fuck you fuck you.'

Everything Is Fine

The worst part was, she was so good at pretending everything was fine, it actually started seeming like everything was fine.

Outwardly, their relationship appeared to be mending, strengthening – Ellery said sorry for being snappy lately and Julia invented reasons of her own to apologise.

Their days and nights went on like normal: working together, leisuring together, a seemingly endless procession of small plates at city restaurants.

In her mind, a break-up felt both imminent and impossible. It was something she knew she needed to do – but also, she might never do it.

When they spoke, niceties were all that she could manage. She was being so pleasant, he was probably having the time of his life.

One evening, walking together, he held her hand and swung it back and forth in exaggerated arcs; reluctantly, she laughed.

'Good,' he said, laughing with her. 'We're enjoying ourself.'

Money

As a precautionary measure against immiserating herself, Julia withdrew the minimum amount of cash she knew she'd need to survive through the coming weeks – her account balance now considerably shortfalling the amount she would soon owe Margot in rent.

On the penultimate day of the month, she called her mother to request financial aid – something she generally tried to avoid doing except in emergency cases.

'Hi Ma.'

'My Jewel! Give me one second.' Her mother's voice sounded both distant and raised.

After she'd counted to ten in her head, Julia said, 'Is everything okay?'

'How *are* you?'

'I'm fine. Is everything okay?'

'Everything's great! I'm busy, I'm driving.'

'I can call—'

'No, I mean, I'm busy driving, but not busy-busy. How's the world of fine cuisine?'

Ordinarily mortified by the word 'cuisine', Julia said: 'Yeah, it's good. Listen, Ma, I need to ask you for a money favour.' She imagined her mother's hands at ten and two on the wheel – her good driving posture. 'Ma, are you there?'

'Yes, I'm here.'

'Is it okay to talk about that?' Without requiring any verification, Julia could remotely sense her mother shaking her head. 'Or, we can chat later if you want.'

'I so regret not teaching you to be more responsible with money.'

'Ma.'

'You're just like your sister. You only want the nicest things. You have no idea how to budget your spending. How to save.'

'I'm asking because—'

'The only times I even hear from your sister these days are when she calls me to ask for money.'

'Ma, I didn't know—'

'Oh, how *would* you know. You have no idea how hard things are for me and how easy they are for you.'

'Ma, really. I'm sorry, I—'

'Just tell me how much you need and I'll forward it across. But this is the last time for a long time that I'm going to do this. You're old enough now to use your money like an adult.'

A Restaurant Somewhere Else

One stilly, pre-summer morning on her walk to work, Julia decided she needed to drastically alter the conditions of her life in order to want to keep on living it. Things could not go on any longer the way they had been.

At first, she struggled to consciously frame the thought. Maybe they could stay together until she found a new job? But no: if she was going to have these bad times separately anyway, it only made sense to consolidate them into one single, unbearable experience rather than string them out. To do just half of what she needed to do would constitute a lateral move. Someday – but not today – she would tender her resignation and break up with Ellery at the same time.

But why not today? You wait too long at anything and you lose the momentum to act.

But how can you ever be fully sure? You will never be fully sure.

But the circuit of her life was small, reducible down to humiliatingly few locations and characters, almost all of which she shared with Ellery – think of the effort it would take to discard that life and start over. Think of that.

In the park, trees she had never paid much attention to before were silently communicating with one another via an internet of subterranean mycorrhizae networked throughout the degrading soil. Julia recoiled from the low flightpath of a bird whose actual likelihood of colliding with her head was difficult for her to determine objectively from her first-person perspective. A group of teenagers ghosted by on Swegways – laughing at something as they overtook Julia, possibly her overreaction to the bird.

From emotion or windburn or maybe both, she started getting watery-eyed; the camouflage colours of the park flaring then blurring together.

Having only ever considered leaving in vague, future-tense terms – the thought of doing so usually expiring as swiftly as it'd surfaced – she felt, this morning, like she'd rearrived at the idea from a new and transformative vantage; as though she'd emerged into a familiar location from a side street she at first hadn't recognised.

Could it be that easy? Could this really be it?

Thinking practically now – aligning her feelings with the facts relating to them – she outlined a mental version of what she needed to say and how she might say it. Just tell him the truth: 'Ellery, I—' etc.

Maybe she could wait until the end of her shift? No, she wouldn't be able to get through the day without making it obvious. Maybe she could just leave him by stealth, disappear? No, that would be insane.

The money from her mother would keep her afloat while she looked for another job. She would be able to find a restaurant somewhere else; a place to start again.

Only now did she notice she'd distractedly continued following the circular path delineating the perimeter of the park after having already gotten as far around it as she'd needed to go. She doubled back on herself and headed directly toward Cascine, avoiding walking too close to the quietway Ellery sometimes cycled along to get to work.

She started doubting her motives as she neared the restaurant. Was she just jumping ship the way she always did when the bloom wore off a new romance, repeating an established pattern of bad, possibly toxic habits? No, this wasn't that – a bright line of trust had been crossed.

As she approached the low-rise, semi-historical building containing Cascine, she felt a mounting sense of dread backdropped by her usual sense of generalised anxiety.

God, I will believe in you for literally the entire rest of my life if you make this easy on me.

Then there he was, at close range – before she felt ready to see him – visible indoors from outdoors, sitting solo at a window table amid a downward-hovering dust shower illuminated by a block of high-definition early-morning light; either the person she loved or the person who impersonated a person she loved.

She opened, stepped beyond, then carefully closed behind her the restaurant's frosted-glass front door – full wash of sun blonding the dining area – preparing to ramp her thoughts into actions. After this last time, I will never set foot in here again. I will no longer live inside your very small idea of me.

He was working on some paperwork, still unaware of Julia's presence; head inclined to an angle that revealed the bald spot the size of a child's palm at the vertex of his scalp; expression affectless, blank as the inside of a mask.

Looking at him, her former anger started to soften into something milder; a signal that had previously been clear to her was steadily losing its strength.

One stilly, pre-summer morning, she could stand by the doorway the entire rest of her life and he might never look up at her. Not until she announced herself, said his name. Four or five paces separated her body from his; the broad, natural daylight that filled the room and reflected back at her from multiple surfaces as glare was almost too much to take. And as she stood there watching him, waiting for the moment she currently occupied to give way to the moment to come, she felt – well, she couldn't exactly think of the right word for it. Changed.

Better Off Alone

I watched as the city glided by, its high-rises diffusing vague blushes of aircraft-warning light into a translucent evening fog. Certain skyscrapers I considered active personal nemeses; had been watching them closely as my carriage entered a tunnel in whose dark I saw my face and the scowl it contained superimposed over the newly blank window opposing me, my reflection elongated a metre wide by its slightly convex glass.

The carriage carrying me quaked; I felt trainsick from the turbulence. I clamped a shoplifted bottle of supermarket-brand rosé tighter between my thighs, and, remembering that I possessed the ability to do so, exercised my pelvic floor.

Only now that I was already most of the way there did I realise I ought to text Teddy and let him know I was coming, having failed to RSVP at any point over the last few weeks.

'HBD ted! think I will come if cool? are julia or roos there?' The message delivered as I emerged from the tunnel.

A pulsing grey ellipsis, signifying messagecraft on Teddy's end, appeared immediately in the bottom left of my smartphone's screen. I wondered if that meant nobody had shown up yet. 'Thanks!' he texted. Then: 'Tonight?'

I hesitated, and replied: 'yep to your party. think I can come if still ok?'

He replied: 'Thought you werent coming!' Then: 'Yes R is here, Julia working early tomo so cant make.' Then: '*It! Excited to all hang out!!' Then: 'I just thought you werent coming!' Then: 'Cant wait', followed by an indecipherable rebus of emoji.

'great,' I replied, 'if youre sure its alright.'

'Of course ofc cant wait, I just thought you werent coming!!! Glad decision was reversed.'

'a perfect 360. see you soon', I composed, reread, replaced '360' with '180', and sent.

Teddy's parents lived in a high-net-worth, citadel-like exurb of the city whose leafy, evenly paved streets were further enriched by electric-car charging ports and anti-homeless architecture. I alighted the train there, tailgating a senior citizen through a ticket barrier to be received by the neighbourhood's premium-quality silence and private views of un-light-polluted nocturnal sky.

On my maps app, an algorithm calculated a fifteen-minute pedestrian route to the party that I was certain I could outpace. I tracked the blue dot representing my virtual, trilaterated self as it slid across an aerial-perspective scale rendering of my surroundings. When I zoomed out slightly to contextualise my position, the unbuffered space beyond the loaded catchment area of my immediate environment appeared as an uncharted beige grid netted with darker beige lines. I pocketed my smartphone to walk unguided.

I had been to Teddy's parents' house three or four times before, but struggled now to recall its exact whereabouts. Facially, the neighbourhood's new-builds all bore the same prominent, hereditary features: cedar cladding; aluminium bay windows; front doors featuring long, vertical bar handles.

After an hour of drinking lukewarm rosé and circling around indistinguishable culs-de-sac, I reached the driveway to what I was mostly pretty sure was Teddy's parents' house.

I recalled that, when I'd last trodden upon this same gravel, two Teddy's-birthdays ago, I'd done so smilingly, holding hands with Julia – I went on a long thought-tangent remembering all the nice things I missed about her, then collected myself; processing the memory.

Realising that I'd stopped walking, I carried on walking. When I arrived at the front door, I paused for a moment before knocking. I reminded myself of advice I'd read online about how to maximise my likeability

111

– that studies had shown authentic confidence could be reverse-engineered via its practised imitation. I exhaled on my hand and smelled the hand.

Nobody answered the door, which, after a second round of knocks, edged ajar.

In the house's vast concourse of a hallway, maybe twenty people, assembled into fours and fives, drank, talked, semi-danced and laughed – about as many golden stelliform balloons bobbed beneath the ceiling's distant skylight. Unnoticed, I stepped into the party.

I was surrounded by people I didn't recognise, who, I guessed from their accents and clothes, were Teddy's dynastically wealthy private-school friends. Most of them were good-looking, I noticed, or otherwise well dressed enough to compensate for their looks.

A four-to-the-floor rhythm from the living room reverberated against the sound-reflecting surfaces of the hallway, between which and the kitchen I estimated – having scoped out both rooms from their doorsills – a further twenty guests were divided. I swept back through the hallway as discreetly as I could, still recognising no one, and produced my smartphone.

I texted Teddy, texted Roos, wrung tighter the slender neck of the rosé bottle with my non-smartphone-wielding hand. After sending the texts, I kept the device aloft in front of me as a prop to support the illusion of my rich interior life; indication that I, too, had circa forty friends, although none of them were here right now.

Eventually, I pocketed my smartphone, circled the hallway once more, and – violating what could reasonably be said to constitute the boundary of a party guest's welcome – headed upstairs.

Urinating into the sink – which maladaptive coping mechanism I had developed as a child from not wanting my parents to hear me using the toilet in the middle of the night, and out of which habit I was still yet to be shamed, having kept it so effectively concealed for over two decades – I stilled in resistance to the lure of my smartphone. Having caught myself midway through the unconscious hand-to-pocket gesture that cued into the device's retrieval, I felt I had outsmarted every former version of myself who had failed to perceive and interrupt this behavioural loop.

As a reward for having achieved this accomplishment of the will, I equipped my smartphone again from my trouser pocket. I returned to the same few social media platforms I usually visited – every time I did so, it was at least partly to check if social media was as bad as I'd remembered it, which, unfailingly, it was.

Skipping through Teddy's Instagram stories, I received a text from Roos: 'Ur coming?? What time??'

I rested my smartphone on the sink's sideboard while I washed and dried my hands with deluxe hand soap and a towel-rail-heated towel. I finished the last of the rosé; burped for a solid three seconds.

Beneath shrill bathroom lights I couldn't remember having switched on, I glanced at myself in the mirror of Teddy's parents' en suite. By now, I was drunk enough for my vision to blur pleasantly at the sides. I dusted a light talc of dandruff from the collar and shoulder regions of my black sweatshirt.

The bathroom smelled of rosé and sandalwood diffuser, and for no reason that I could have explained if called upon to do so, I search-engined the words: *sandalwood diffuser*. 'Wow,' I said to myself out loud. They were less expensive than I had thought.

Downstairs, I resumed a solitary position, remained a foreign object to the tissue of selves constituting the party's body of guests.

I was heading across the hallway for the kitchen, where the drinks presumably were, when I felt myself being embraced from behind. I turned around while being held and Teddy yelled my name directly into my ear. I hugged him back, and, at regular volume, he said how nice it was to see me.

I wished him a happy birthday, felt fleetingly self-conscious for not having bought him a gift, then lied: 'You're looking seriously great.'

In fact, Teddy was looking seriously worse than I'd ever seen him. Not just worse, but bigger – not just bigger, but iller. His cheekboneless, dairy-product-soft face seemed paler than it had before; the semi-solid of his midsection larger and more set.

A yo-yo dieter to and from whose fluctuating frame the same four stone had been added and subtracted for the duration of his adult life, Teddy had evidently spent the last few months in a sustained phase of bodily expansion. I recalled that, over the entire course of our friendship at and post-university, I had seen Teddy shirtless only the once, changing out of heavily rained-on clothes years ago – I pictured again the forlornly face-like configuration of his nipples and bellybutton as I had seen them on that day.

That mental image slowly disintegrated as we said more and more friendly things to each other; exchanged slaps on the back; made references to old times.

I felt the familiar lift of being in his company; I knew we loved each other a lot. Teddy asked if I'd had any-thing to drink yet and when I said no, he grabbed my cheek and said, 'Well, we'll have to do something about that, won't we.'

In the lowlit, densely peopled kitchen, Teddy introduced me to Héloïse, who in turn introduced me to Lior, whom I introduced back to Teddy.

'Of course I know Lior,' Teddy said, as though this were a matter of public record; 'Lior's father works with my father, and they're both extremely important people.'

This, I now remembered, was in fact long-established friendship-canon: Teddy and Lior's fathers co-owned a firm that had to do with architecture or law or architectural law, and worse, I was in the process of remembering, Lior and I had met several times previously at club nights and bar nights whose transport and, where necessary, ticket-purchase logistics Teddy had arranged. Lior's face tensed into a smile I recognised – from other, more familiar faces I'd disappointed – as one that was merely decorative.

'Sweetie,' Teddy said, the right of his dependably warm hands covering the left of my poorly oxygenated and permanently cold own, 'be a sweetie and get us something good from the fridge?'

Grateful to have been assigned a task that required me to exit the conversation, I slouched off toward the fridge and opened its giant stainless-steel door.

116

On a shelf at my exact eye level, twelve varietals of white wine stood in formation four bottles across by three rows deep. The bottles all looked to be straining their necks taller out of eagerness to be chosen; I read their labels by fridgelight, scanning for any recognisable hall-mark of quality, twiddling my fingers before tentatively picking the Frenchest-sounding one, replacing it, then selecting the bottle beside it and returning to Teddy.

He handed me a battery-powered corkscrew that looked like a police torch, and I said, positioning the device around the neck and down to the shoulders of the bottle, 'Are you sure this'll work?' to which he replied it would. I noticed his smartphone, a practically nov-elty-sized device that barely fit in one hand, held at an awkward angle in front of his chest, trained on me. 'Are you filming?' I asked, to which he again responded in the affirmative. After I had successfully applied the utensil to the bottle and received applause for wresting the cork from its neck, he added something inaudible to me that made everyone else laugh.

I decanted the wine among a septet of spare sinkside glasses that I realised too late were not actually spare glasses but in fact used and unwashed ones, considered rinsing at least their outsides with detergent but didn't, then distributed the replenished, highly bacterial glasses among the host and his surrounding guests.

117

Teddy scarved my shoulders with one arm and reiterated how glad he was to see me. His teeth purpled from red wine and his breath soured from white wine, he raised his voice to recite to his audience an anecdote I'd heard so many times I could remember where its pauses for laughter came. (I had worried, then felt embarrassed for having worried, that he was first going to raise a toast to me.) When he finished, I considered telling my own tangentially related anecdote, doubted its applicability, and, by the time I had deemed it worthy of retelling, realised its window of relevance to the current conversation had closed.

I drank my drink quickly, refilled it, drank my next drink even quicker, then pushed my empty glass an arm's-length away from me across the kitchen island. I had a good buzz going now, smiling around at all Teddy's friends, who were also starting to feel like they were my friends.

I wondered briefly if something was really wrong with me, or if things were only a little bit wrong with me, like with everyone else. Then I shifted thoughts to the four-to-the-floor rhythm that was still just audible from the living room, toward which I headed in search of Roos.

Who must have felt the weight of my attention settle upon her, as no sooner had I left the kitchen than I heard her calling my name from across the hallway.

'Hey stranger,' she said, nearing into me amid a crowd of the young and upwardly mobile. She was, bravely, the only person at the party wearing summer-weight clothes.

We hugged hello. 'Howdy,' I said, and immediately regretted.

'It's been a while,' she said, which was true.

Roos and I used to be a lot closer than we currently were. Back when we both worked purgatorial, under-paid desk jobs, we'd hung out every weekend, but since then our fortunes had diverged – she'd lucked into a 'cool media career' through a boyfriend of a friend, upgraded living situations into a sitcom-sized apartment in a pricier zone of the city, and now I barely saw her.

She was laughing at my face, which I could feel had gone slack from booze. 'You look like you're having the total time of your life.'

'I am having a good time,' I insisted, forcing myself to smile.

At some point, a beer had manifested in my hand – maybe Roos planted it there, I didn't want to ask. I wondered if I should sober up to base reality before continuing to drink, then took a few long glugs anyway while she was looking in another direction.

'I can never quite believe this house,' she said, shaking her head in disbelief. 'Can you believe this house?'

I wiped my lips with the back of my hand. 'It's unbelievable.'

Roos cocked her head to the side. 'No Julia tonight.'

'Oh. Yeah.'

'When'd you last see her?'

I thought for a second. 'Years.'

'Y'know she's seeing some old guy?'

'What?'

'She's dating some old guy.'

'Who?'

'Julia.'

There was no time for this. 'What old guy?'

'Her boss, or something. He's middle-aged.'

'She told you this?'

'No, she told Teddy. And Teddy's obviously a blimp, secret-keeping-wise.'

'Well,' I said, looking down, 'good for them, I guess.' Roos was wearing a silver ring on one of her index toes, but I didn't have the heart to make fun of her for it now.

'Y'know who is here, though?' she said. 'Stanislaw Richter.'

'Stanis—?'

'—law Richter. Remember him? He was, like, the coolest guy in third year.'

'*Stanislaw Richter*,' I said affirmatively, nodding, not recalling the name. 'What's he doing here?'

'Friends with Teddy, I guess. He's super-rich now, off stocks or something.'

'Isn't everyone here rich?'

'Not you,' Roos said. Then, conscientiously, 'Nor me.'

'Well, maybe if you fall in love with a rich guy,' I said, then threw back the rest of my beer.

She gave me a tolerant look. 'Y'know what else?'

'No.'

'It's nice to see you,' she said, patting the top of my head. Slowly, she retracted her hand. 'When was the last time you washed your hair?'

Through the living room, a set of eight panoramic glass bifold doors had been concertinaed open to allow guests to circulate outside.

Roos and I were on the patio with fresh drinks, mingling. Somehow, Roos wasn't cold, although I was freezing, standing with my arms folded and hands under my armpits, conserving heat.

Facing away from the house, it was dark enough that I had to concentrate to see; my pupils, I guess, were dilating. I could just about make out the male speaker to whom Roos had (and I hadn't) been listening for some time. Only when I heard him use the words 'escrow' and 'volatility' in the same sentence did I realise he must be Stanislaw Richter.

He didn't seem to comprehend that Roos was more interested in him personally than in hearing about his cryptocurrency investments. Whenever she laughed at one of his stories, he followed it up with another, longer one containing even finer details about his virtual day-trades.

By the time Stanislaw produced his smartphone to demonstrate an app depicting live graphs and tabulated market indices relating to his digital-coin portfolio – tipping the device sideways several times to reorient its display to landscape – I felt the need, for all our sakes, to interrupt and change the subject.

'And what is it you do again, Roos?' I said, mocking her in advance for the way she explained her job to people.

'*I facilitate partnerships between creatives and multinationals to help artists elevate their voices and brands reach wider audiences,*' she recited, eyes closed, from a job description in her head.

'And what about you?' Stanislaw said, looking at me.

How to explain to someone I had just heard enumerating his multiple passive income streams that I wrote copy for minimum wage at a failing marketing firm; was broke; lived on minus money in an overdraft that was almost overdrawn? 'I do basically nothing,' I said.

Stanislaw laughed.

'No, really,' I said.

Usually when I was this drunk I performed only the minimum number of actions required of me, so as not to make any preventable mistakes or draw undue attention to myself. Now, to appear relaxed, I decided to rest my foot on the seat of a wicker lawn chair positioned between Stanislaw and Roos. After I'd assumed this unnecessary posture, preparing to continue to speak, I felt the chair scraping out from under my foot and my body free-falling forward.

Stanislaw caught me immediately, but I took several additional seconds to properly regain my balance. I kept apologising and explaining my error to him: 'I misjudged the weight, or whatever. The support.'

'It's fine,' Stanislaw said, his grip firm around my arm.

'Are you okay?' Roos asked, multiple times, using adjusted formatting of phrase.

I was fine, I was good, I was really alright, 'The chair was just lighter than I'd guessed.'

Suddenly, it seemed imperative to prove to them that I wasn't drunk at all – that all was well and the night still held good things in store for me. For us.

In the background, I heard the extremely loud, low-end bass of Alice Deejay's 'Better Off Alone' coming from the living room – a song I historically neither liked nor disliked, but which now seemed to possess untold depths of feeling; could possibly make me cry.

I looked at the lawn chair lying on its back, then at Stanislaw and Roos. 'You guys wanna dance?' I said.

Roos and I took to a corner of the dance floor as a pair, Stanislaw having respectfully declined my invitation.

Roos danced like a woman in an advert for probiotic yogurt, and for a short but exhilarating time I was able to imitate confidence into existence and dance along with her.

She loved this song, I think she said, her words aimed not at me but at the room's farthest corners, and I was happy, and forgot myself, and she smiled so fully it looked like the start of a scream.

After eight more choruses across three separate songs, I became gradually aware of having begun to move my body manually as opposed to automatically, as though whatever propulsive force I'd entrusted to animate my limbs for the dance's duration had abandoned them midway through the act.

Panicking, I outswung and retracted my arms in a series of bird-like, arrhythmic gestures I then attempted to retroactively stylise and add symmetry to via methodical repetition into what you might describe as a kind of Charleston or maybe a floss.

I looked over at Roos, who I was relieved to find – having federated our dance partnership with several neighbouring dance partnerships to form a wider dance collective (including, among others, Teddy and Lior) – too busy seizing the moment to notice I had forgotten how to move in time to music.

Once the next chorus was underway, I lost all sense of bodily momentum. I shambled over to the dance floor's sidelines, where I stood smilingly observing the scene for just long enough to start feeling like a creep – then considered that I probably *was* a creep with all my problems, schemes and self-pity – and subsequently emerged into the kitchen wondering what it must feel like to be not only not a creep but also in love with one's own body and, by extension, in love with the immediate spheres of world with which that body came into contact.

I leant against something horizontal and picked up a half-empty, discarded flute of sparkling white wine, watched chains of bubbles effervesce toward its surface, threw it back, refilled the emptied glass with some to-hand Maker's Mark, and repeated.

I focused on the clock above the sink, whose face displayed a time both earlier and later than seemed possible. I closed my eyes for a moment and when I reopened them and looked back up at the clock, another five minutes had passed.

Roos Rees-Anderson, swimming in a ladies-only outdoor pool.

Below that: Roos eating chia pudding from a Mason jar in black and white; Roos and two friends wearing athleisure clothes before or after running in a city park; Teddy posing in flattering café light with a matcha green latte; a still life of a bestselling work of popular anthropology.

My smartphone's display mounted twelve at a time of the thousand-plus other tiles archiving moments of suchlike activity in Roos's life; I scrolled through them in a series of accelerating thumbstrokes.

I was back in Teddy's parents' en suite bathroom; once again, I had no memory of switching on the room's overhead light.

I located and pinch-zoomed into a picture of Roos, Teddy, Julia and I taken a couple of years ago at a previous iteration of the same party as tonight. I released the photo, then navigated to Teddy's recently updated Instagram story, wherefrom I was startled to hear my own voice emitting outside my body via the footage he'd recorded of me earlier uncorking a wine bottle using unfamiliar technology. 'Are you filming?' The bottle opened, the video blurred, and, over applause, Teddy announced: 'I'll have what he's having!'

I drank another finger from the bottle of Maker's. When I got a good enough momentum going, no amount of negative reinforcement could halt my drinking; I would carry on, without let-up, until I blacked out.

I knew that, soon, I would need to do something about this; change my habits and stop making the same mistakes over and over.

For years, I'd promised myself I'd get it together and start writing. Based on very little evidence, I had a feeling I would someday be capable of writing something good. I'd finished a few short stories for a creative writing class back at university and had, at some point, shown them to Julia – I remembered her saying how much she'd liked them. In fact, my grade for that module had been the highest I'd received in my entire degree.

My problem was, I couldn't force myself to do the things I wanted to do; couldn't make myself start writing any more than I could make myself stop drinking. Some self-sabotaging mechanism in my personality derailed my every attempt to make positive changes in my life.

In order to start making those changes, I reasoned, I would have to undergo some kind of pre-change change; become the kind of person who could readily make such changes. But how was I even supposed to make that initial, pre-change change? Let alone the many incremental micro-changes I would first have to make on the way to making a pre-pre-change change?

Thinking about all those changes, I climbed into

Teddy's parents' empty bathtub, within which I continued to intermittently sip from the Maker's, and where I remained still enough and long enough for the room's motion-sensitive light to eventually tick back off, lapsing my surroundings into darkness.

I awoke to a familiar, almond-sized locus of pain zinging beneath my scalp. I was so drunk, all I could think about was how drunk I was.

The rest of the party I experienced as a succession of non-continuous tableaux, slides changing without transition.

I knocked on and craned my head around Teddy's bedroom door, witnessed him, shirted, big-spooning a shirtless Lior – the two of them folded into one another as neatly as stacked classroom chairs. I considered waking them to ask if Roos was still in the house, but didn't.

Relieved of its guests, whose collective bodily warmth still lingered in their absence, the downstairs hallway seemed to have expanded, as if it had finally breathed out.

I barged into, ran a quick mental diagnostic on, and promptly reversed back out of the living room, whose dance floor had been vacated save for Héloïse and someone I didn't know, then headed straight through to the kitchen, where Stanislaw and Roos were sitting on a sofa talking about decentralised markets – their legs close together but not touching.

'Chief,' Stanislaw said, noticing me, being either very nice or condescendingly nice. 'All good?'

'Never better,' I said, refocusing my eyeline toward him after it had drifted off-centre.

Roos got up and drew me a glass of tap water, which I acted like was uncalled for but did drink. 'Are you staying here?' she said.

'Yes,' I said, my vision reeling from a bad case of the spins. Then, in a voice that I did not at first recognise as my own: 'No. I just want to go home.'

In spite of late-night surge pricing and broader ethical concerns I had surrounding the company's existence at large, I allowed Stanislaw to book me an Uber back from the party. When it arrived he placed me in the back seat, protecting my head with his hand like he was making a gentle arrest, and as we said goodbye I thanked him as impassively as I could, like I was doing him the favour.

Later, Maksim, the cab's driver, asked what I had been up to that night. My Uber rating crossed my mind, and I slurred that I had gone to a party, then enunciated more carefully that I had danced with a beautiful girl there.

'Nice,' Maksim said.

'Yeah. It is nice,' I said, belatedly putting together that it was Stanislaw's Uber rating and not my own at stake. I resolved to do nothing to jeopardise his current standing in the eyes of the ridesharing corporation.

Residential streets rushed by the rear passenger-side window against which my left cheek rested; eventually, all those municipal roads fused into dual carriageway. I felt the childhood oceanic feeling of being sleepy in the back seat of a safely driven car at night.

At some point, the female TomTom voice telling Maksim where to go said, 'Turn left in four hundred metres.'

Maksim gestured to the device and said, 'I hate this cunt.'

I instructed Maksim to let me out after a further five minutes of driving. He said was I sure and I said yes, and as I watched the red and gold lights of his car fade into darkness I realised I had no idea where I was.

I produced my smartphone and opened my chat with Teddy, returning to the conversation we had been having, across mixed media, for almost a decade. 'did u fuck lior??' I composed into white space, before replacing 'fuck' with 'bone' with 'smash', laughing, and deleting the whole message. 'text in the morning x', I rewrote and sent. 'tell stan thanks for the lift', I wrote to Roos and deleted.

I sang aloud the titular line to 'Better Off Alone', real-ised those were the only words I knew of the song, then realised that they were also almost the song's only lyrics, and sang them over several more times. I located myself on my maps app and received directions home.

Before heading up to the apartment, I purchased, ate, and burned the roof of my mouth on a family-sized peppero-ni pizza, then vomited it back up in slice-by-slice bursts against the outer plexiglass panel of a roadside bus shelter.

I arrived home to find my bedroom light on and door wide open, which I freaked out about for a moment before remembering I'd left them that way myself.

Drunk, with an aftertaste of bile in my mouth, I wept watching the too-beautiful rising sun redden the dawn cityscape beyond my bedroom window. Trace verticals of rain began to fall, connecting everything intrinsic to my life to everything extrinsic from it: Teddy; Roos; Stanislaw; Maksim; Julia out there somewhere; the apricot-coloured smear of vomit I'd left on the bus shelter; every pavement on which I'll ever walk to work.

Then, because I was feeling nostalgic, I withdrew my smartphone and checked out Julia's Facebook profile.

Julia had by far the least active online presence of any-one my own age whom I considered to be of priority-tier significance to my life. No outward evidence suggested she'd logged into her Facebook account in years, although, I supposed, it was possible she had. The upload date of her current profile picture preceded by an entire semester even our first meeting on campus, which had occurred at a nineties-themed mixer in the students' union bar toward the end of both our fresher years. I had attended the night with Teddy, whom I'd met in halls and clung to closely since he was good at making friends. Julia, meanwhile, had arrived in a convoy of her already-drunk geography coursemates, who were celebrating finishing their exams.

Late into the night, I was sitting alone in a booth listening to Selena, finishing the fishbowl of blue drink Teddy had ordered for us to share moments before he'd gone home with a varsity hockey player.

A girl I didn't know came over and sat down beside me – the realisation of a fantasy that I imagined literally every time I went out.

'Hi,' she said, looking right at me, and, without breaking eye contact, leant over and guppied her lips around the rim of my fishbowl, searching for a straw. After she'd managed to sip a few strawfuls, she grimaced up at me and asked what kind of cocktail this was.

'Electric lemonade,' I said.

'Amazing,' she said, and took another, longer sip.

'Are you with all those people?' I said, gesturing with

my forehead toward the loose-knit but still distinct group of students from which I'd seen her emerge.

'Depends what you mean by "with", but yeah, I am,' she said, and added, '*the geographers*,' in a tone that derided the group but in a still affectionate way.

She put her arm around me then asked for my name. 'Nick,' I said, and extended a hand in her direction. She looked at it. 'To shake with,' I said, and we awkwardly shook hands.

We stared at each other for a moment and eventually kissed. 'I'm Roos,' she said, after.

From the corner of my eye, then with my full two eyes, I saw a new girl dancing over toward us, also from the geography group. I knew Roos was watching me watching her, but she didn't seem to mind, and anyway I couldn't help it.

We both changed postures as the girl danced nearer; Roos sitdown-danced back at her while I straightened up in my seat.

'Who's that?' I said.

'Who, her?' Roos said, raising her voice so it reached the new girl, beginning our introduction. 'That's Julia.'

*Distraction from Sadness Is Not
the Same Thing as Happiness*

The algorithm took into consideration the common interests, venning friendships and left-to-right swipe-ratio-categorised attractiveness brackets of the two users before providing each with the other's profile card for approval.

At 19:15 BST, which by now the algorithm had determined to be her peak time of app usage, the female user sat in one of the give-up seats at the front of a single-deck city bus, and, via the interface of her smartphone's algorithm-based dating app, encountered the male user's profile card for the first time.

Upon seeing his profile card (which, like the rigidly customisable profile cards of the algorithm-based dating app's other non-premium users, consisted starkly of a forename- and age-bearing header; a scrollable gallery of six 500-x-500px square images; and, below that, a geographical location marker plus maximum five lines of introductory sans-serif text), the female user close-to-instantly registered that the male user was the exact type of guy she (and the algorithm) would classify as 'her type'.

The algorithm took note of the haste with which the female user scrolled through, then back a second time through, the pictures of the male user; the celerity with which she accordingly swiped right on his profile card, constituting, by a comfortable margin, a record decision-making time for a user otherwise grouped into the algorithm's upper-eightieth percentile for choosiness.

After presenting to the female user a rendering of the word 'LIKE' being stamped diagonally across the male user's forehead, the algorithm dissolved his profile card from the dating app's main display and generated a full-screen dynamic ad intended to appeal to the female user by promoting a product relevant to her known wants and spending behaviours. In the case of the female user specifically, said product was a cosmetic cream manufactured to tighten loose or flabby skin below the mandible.

Midway through the ad's eighteen-second playtime, the female user clicked her smartphone locked and stared out of the nearest bus window. Whether or not she absently ran the backs of her fingers over the soft underside of her chin as she watched the passing world and considered her place in it, the algorithm could not say.

The male user – supine, abed, and whose peak time of app usage was occurring now, some six hours later than that of the female user – came across her profile card mid-deck, roughly thirty profile cards deep into his late-night swiping binge. The algorithm arranged these encounters strategic-ally, needling a user's most-statistically-likely matches into the dense haystacks of their least-statistically-likely matches in order to prolong the stretches of unbroken, habit-forming, in-app time spent by its users.

As the male user observed the female user's profile, so too did the algorithm observe him; surveilled the way he, predictably, paused longest on her lone bikini pic while cycling through the cloud-stored images retrieved from the algorithm-based dating app's central image database, whose actual physical servers were located four-thousand-plus transatlantic miles from the male and female users' city of mutual residence. The male user concentrated long enough on the image of the female user to begin feeling confined by it.

In full knowledge of the enterprise's probable futili-ty, but without anything else to do before he slept, the male user conducted a few cursory social media and pro-fessional networking site searches of the female user's first name followed by select speechmarked keywords relating to her profession and alma mater copied from her bio, the only available clues as to her identity, none of which yielded any relevant results. Then he thumbed back to the algorithm-based dating app's main interface and swiped right on the female user's profile.

That swipe prompted the cursive-style words 'It's A

Match!' to appear in the centre of the male user's smartphone while, simultaneously, two circles, each containing one of the two users' main profile images, rolled to a halt mid-screen beneath the bannered text – a combination of words and images which always, without fail, prompted the male user to involuntarily hear the *Looney Tunes* 'That's All Folks!' closing theme reverberating from some backroom inside his head.

Having received the gut-situated upsurge of jackpot-style gratification that attaining a new match still provided him, the male user sat up a little on his single-extra-sized mattress. Hoping to use the satiated feeling of having reached a desired outcome with little to no effort as a kind of emotional forcefield through which to venture into emotional territories ordinarily too painful for him to brave, the male user circled back through his most recently used apps and, via his smartphone's web browser, revisited one of the social media sites on which he'd just attempted to identify the female user.

The male user proceeded to type the full name of his most recent long-term sexual partner into the social media site's top-level search bar and, finding her there, monitored the activity displayed on her personal feed. He scanned through a few new tagged photos in which she looked like she'd put on weight; combed the names of certain profiles she'd recently interacted with; skim-read

140

a fundraising page for a child's specialist medical bills she'd shared.

Still revolving the idea of his most recent long-term sexual partner in his head, the male user navigated to his go-to pornography site and masturbated for six minutes while watching a pornographic video on mute. He masturbated neither to the pornography itself nor to the thoughts of his most recent long-term sexual partner, but instead to an imagined, holographic-seeming emulsion of the two separate stimuli: his most recent long-term sexual partner's face overlaying the porn actress's body, then the porn actress's face overlaying his most recent long-term sexual partner's body. It felt relaxing and automatic to do this.

Afterward, he speculated about how depressing he must look to the walls, to God, to the algorithm, to any of his deceased family members if they were watching him the way he imagined them, crystal-ball-style from the bright white halls of the afterlife.

Although the algorithm knew exactly how the male user frittered his time, it was incapable of passing judgement on him. It reassured the male user to remind himself that none of this software had any vested interest in him personally; that it basically only existed to furnish him with ads.

Next morning, within a minute of her smartphone's bird-like alarm sounding beneath her pillow, the female user opened the algorithm-based dating app to be greeted by the same congratulatory match notification that the male user had received seven hours earlier.

After viewing the 'It's A Match!' animation, the female user (again, at a pace of substantial variance to her usual browsing speed) returned to the male user's profile card, now situated in her new-matches chatlist, and carouselled once more through the six images he'd uploaded to the app. She had a good feeling, felt the arc of her life bending, however forcedly, into alignment with the life of a perfect stranger.

Later that day, on his lunch hour which was really only ever a half-hour because he wanted to be taken more seriously around the office, the male user thumbprinted his smartphone unlocked and opened the algorithm-based dating app with the barely registered intention of beginning an interaction with the female user.

With the bulk reserves of his attention allocated toward other things, the male user absently copied, from a previous conversation with a different female user in his new-matches chatlist, the same opening line he'd used on almost all of his algorithm-based dating app matches so far, and pasted it into the vacant text box directly below the latest female user's forename and main profile image.

Having waited a requisite number of hours after receiving the male user's message so as to appear sufficiently busy and not desperately alone, the female user pieced together a response to the male user that sounded both playful and hedging.

In the break area of her co-working space, she mouthed the message aloud to herself as she ticked it out on her smartphone's touchscreen keyboard, her face sunbatherly in the absence of conveyed emotion.

The female user enjoyed the clean, asensual experience of using the algorithm-based dating app; the position of freedom and control, of distance, afforded to her by its streamlined simulation of encounter and romance. She liked that it was low-risk, easy to weed out the creeps and easy to unmatch from those who later revealed themselves to be creeps; liked that its shielding, one-way-mirror mechanism meant she never had to commit the harm of rejecting anyone to their face, nor suffer the indignity of ever being rejected directly to hers.

Naturally, when it came to venturing beyond the protections of the virtual world, it was easy for the female user to foresee her own violent death at the hands of one of her matches. Even with the safeguards of being able to snoop on and correspond indefinitely with a male user before consenting to meet him, every one of the female user's eight previous app-arranged first dates had prompted her to ideate, for days in advance, over being brutally beaten, raped or (as per her foremost current concern) acid-attacked by a potential suitor.

In the week that followed, the two users exchanged thirty-five total messages spanning the standard big-three Wikipedia-entry subhead topics of early life, career and personal life. Finding their outward-facing personalities to be compatible, the users traded numbers and arranged to meet at a bar in an only recently gentrified area of the city within a quarter-mile of equidistance to their two places of work.

Both users had patronised the venue in the past, but, for reasons not entirely clear to her, the female user pretended to the male user, both in their messages arranging the in-person encounter and for the full duration of the in-person encounter itself, that she had never previously attended the bar.

The female user disappointed herself when she did things like this, which was often. Lying ran directly counter to her moral ideal of how a person should act in the world. In fact, when judging others, the female user counted honesty as her highest-priority virtue.

She couldn't say with any accuracy when she'd become such a fluent liar. Her lies were never really thought out – the same way nothing she ever said was – which was probably the reason why she generally preferred to communicate via text than speech; a calculative solution to the comparatively freehand and chaotic risks of person-to-person interaction. A means of revising the kind of a person she was.

The anticipation of enjoyment is a feeling texturally similar to dread. Their date loomed over the female user's week like a deadline.

Walking to the agreed-upon venue, the female user worried that she might struggle to generate conversation in the evening ahead. She reiterated several times to herself her overall strategy for the date, which was to present to the male user an exaggeratedly carefree, pretty, lite-version of her real self; a person-shaped suite of attractive gestures and responses whose outline she could gradually, somewhere down the line, restock with elements of the personality she actually had.

She discovered the male user outside the bar, seated on the lid of a yellow container of grit salt. He was clad in generic menswear and engrossed by something on his smartphone.

'Hi?' the female user said, earphones popping from her ears as she wound their connecting Y-cord around her smartphone.

The male user looked up from his device and took a moment to parse the specifics of the female user's face; the way her hair, lighter and shorter than in any of her pictures, fell in two khaki-coloured wings on either side of her chin. She bore a resemblance to someone the male user had seen before but couldn't place, perhaps from real life or a film or pornography, or maybe just from the pictures on her profile.

'How's it going,' the male user said, standing. At full height he was, miraculously, three-ish inches taller than the female user had expected.

'Good, I'm sorry I'm late,' the female user said, her voice lower than the male user had imagined, as if concealing a yawn. 'I got the bus but there was a thing with a guy on it and we got held up. Should we—' The female user gestured *go inside* in a way that made her hands feel lonesome.

The two users entered the bar – the female user conscious not to over- or under-act the specific facial cast of a person taking in an interior entirely new to them. A popular song that featured prominently in the advertising campaign for a model of car aimed toward the millennial market was streaming over the bar's sound system; the male user's embarrassment at this was noticeable and off-putting to the female user.

'It's pretty busy in here,' the female user said, raising her voice clear of the music. 'Is it always this busy?'

'It's definitely gotten more popular,' the male user said, grimacing. 'But we can go outside. There's this kinda beer garden thing.'

'Okay. Yeah. Okay. You see if there's any spaces and I'll wait at the, uh—'

'Yeah,' the male user said. 'Or actually, how about you go get us a space and I'll get us both drinks. It's just through there, past those double doors. What d'you normally have?'

'Sure?'

'Yeah.'

'Well, for now I'll just have what you're having.'

'Okay,' the male user said. 'A Guinness with a raw egg in it.'

'My usual.' The female user heel-pivoted around in a way she'd practised, then headed through to the outside area.

It was warm out; the summer, only recently concluded, had left in its wake a two-week coda of placid heat like a parting gift. The female user sat down at the empty

147

side of a long, half-busy table, the populated end of which accommodated a group of anthropometrically near-perfect, glossy-looking girls whose presence made the female user feel medium-sized and matte-finished by comparison.

A memory bobbed to the surface of the female user's thoughts: a former algorithm-based dating app match telling her she was 'homely', which he had intended, he later tried to explain, as a compliment.

After the female user had taken the opportunity to feel bad about her weight and rearrange her body in a way she hoped appeared attractive and relaxed, the male user came out of the bar with a glass of beer in each hand. He looked limited and pathetic carrying the two drinks and shimmying his way toward her, so much so that she pretended not to have seen him until he set their glasses on the table.

'This does not look like my usual.'

'I asked. They were all out of eggs.'

'I'm never coming here again. Thank you.'

There was a comfortable, anticipatory silence as the two users took sips of their beers, which were warm and sepia-coloured and had an aftertaste of medicine. Then the silence lasted too long and became uncomfortable.

'So, how was your day?'

'It was good,' the female user said. '*Fun*,' she added, the word italicised by her tone.

'That's good,' the male user said. 'Most people I know hate their jobs.'

'Do you hate your job?'

'I try not to hate stuff if I can avoid it.'

'That's *brave*,' the female user said, doing the thing with her voice again.

'I don't consider it all that brave,' the male user said.

A gale of laughter sounded from the far end of the table; the attractive girls were huddled together around one of their smartphones. The female user considered that she should be laughing more to put the male user at ease.

The two users sipped their drinks.

'Do you smoke?' the female user said.

'Uh, I mean, not in any sustained way.'

'*Not in any sustained way*,' she repeated.

The male user courtesy-laughed at this but felt wounded by the female user's impression of him. He was finding it difficult to gauge her feelings toward him generally, or to know if she even experienced the having of feelings the same way he did. 'What I mean is, I smoked all the way through school and then for a couple of years after that, but then it started making me anxious. Like, when I'd go to sleep I'd start thinking about all the slush in my lungs, all the sludge and the tar, and then I wouldn't be able to stop thinking about all those pictures of cadavers and babies with harelips on the packets. So I just had to stop.

149

Smoking. But I mean, I'll still smoke sometimes. If I'm with people and they're smoking, I'll probably have one.'

As he spoke, the female user traced the reassuring, talismanic contours of her smartphone through her trouser pocket. 'What you mean is, you're just waiting for someone to enable you and you haven't really quit at all.'

'Exactly.'

The female user produced a pouch of tobacco and said, 'Well, it sounds like you've made a very healthy choice,' and the male user laughed and said, 'Yeah, I make a lot of those.'

In a second bar, which appeared not to be part of a chain but in fact was, the two users continued to drink and perform to each other the versions of themselves they hoped someday to be. The female user laughed at the male user's theory about how he could prevent getting a hangover by sticking to one brand of beer for the whole night and the male user laughed at anecdotes the female user had plagiarised from friends.

The female user spilled nervous talk over any threat of silence and several times had the feeling of having overshared. At one point, she quoted out loud a motivational post about happiness and its relation to distraction she'd read on an image-sharing social media site earlier that day. The way the male user raised his eyebrows and nodded after she'd said it made the female user feel unembarrassed and understood.

By the time they reached a third bar, the male user had become drunk enough to have, several times, completely lost the thread of their conversation; the female user had to close one eye to keep from seeing double.

The female user liked the male user, she'd decided, and waited for him to put the moves on her. Several times, as they walked close together in the dense night heat, his hand or leg brushed against hers.

Just when the female user had become fully certain the male user wasn't going to make any kind of physical advance toward her, he did. His lips tasted of leading-brand lip balm.

After the female user had boarded her bus home, the male user took a taxi back to his. In bed, he considered texting the female user something like: 'Did you get home safely?' He decided against this.

On their second date, the two users spent six minutes engaged in eye contact; consumed five rounds of drinks; encountered more than three-hundred ambient, native and overt advertisements combined; were proximal to fourteen persons suffering chronic pain, eleven Christs in statuary.

At some point, the male user asked the female user if she believed in life after death. He looked scared talking about it, and the female user wondered momentarily if he was terminally ill. She pictured sitting at the male user's bedside as he underwent chemotherapy, then imagined speaking at his funeral, his head lunar-bald, visible from an open casket.

It was hard for her to say exactly why she liked the male user so much. He was good-looking, but there was something else; a single-facetedness and fixed sense of himself she found magnetic. As if everything he did was joined up. His gait, his way of talking, his mannerisms – all connected.

'No, I don't think I believe in an afterlife,' the female user said. Some people just smell like home.

'I'm changing my answer. I think maybe I do believe in life after death.'

'really? this is huge. what prompted this?'

'We'll thinking about dying mainly.' Moments later, she added: '*well.'

'haha. I hope there is an afterlife. I think about dying almost all the time.'

'Sounds deep.'

'I am deep.' Later, when she was watching her shows, he followed up with: 'do you have weekend plans?'

'How old are you again?' she said after.

'I think you'll find it says on my profile.'

'Twenty-six?'

'Twenty-seven.'

'An old man practically.'

'I know. I feel like an old man. I feel like I'm at the age where my life should start, like, solidifying into its permanent shape.'

'I think you'll feel that way at every age. But, I'm twenty-five for another two months, so what do I know.'

'That's a big one.'

'What?'

'What.'

'What's a big one?'

'Turning twenty-six. It was a big deal for me. I really freaked out when I turned twenty-six. A gateway year. Things start getting serious from there.'

'I think I'll save my worrying for when I turn twenty-seven.'

'Why? Because that's the age where your life should start solidifying into its permanent shape? Or because of the thing? The club.'

'The club. I don't think life has a shape.'

'Kurt Cobain. Jimi Hendrix.'

153

'Amy Winehouse.'

'New *Star Trek* guy.'

'Janis Joplin.' The female user shifted her legs slightly under the covers. 'All yours are men, by the way.'

'Brian Wilson.'

'Brian Wilson is alive, I've seen him play the Beach Boys. And also, he's another man.'

'I know, I meant the other Brian. Brian someone else. It's the last age where you can still die young. And I think my examples are all men mainly because the culture has an innate, like, bias that way. Not because I'm, me specifically, being sexist about it.'

The female user nodded, which – realising the male user couldn't see her – she verbalised as: 'Sure.' In the swimming dark of the room, she couldn't remember what the male user actually looked like, only the images from his profile. 'You're wrong, but sure.'

'How am I wrong?' The male user rolled onto his side so their voices faced.

'Because, that's not how that kind of a thing works.'

'Well, okay then. I'm sure I can name a woman who died when she was twenty-seven if you *really* want me to.'

'No, that isn't the point,' the female user said, resting an arm heavily over the male user's shoulder. He could hear the smile in her voice.

Nights, the female user filmed herself. Her routine was to set her laptop on a stack of pillows on her bed and tilt its screen to where she was most fully visible to its camera. Then she would launch the laptop's photo-capturing software, begin recording a video and step several paces away from the device to mime having a conversation, or listening, or laughing – any naturalistic activity she might soon perform in public. She rehearsed small, choreographed movements before the laptop's lens. Knowing she was being watched, she behaved more carefully.

The female user would then lie in bed and spend tens of minutes, whole halves of hours, watching replays of the recorded footage. She would watch until she felt disembodied from the body onscreen, until that body felt thing-like and virtual.

Watching the videos over, the female user paid close attention to each of her embarrassing human surfaces, the resting bloat of her stomach or slight listing of her posture; noting everything she needed to improve. She was working on herself, upgrading by increments. Basically only trying to look special.

'https://en.wikipedia.org/wiki/27_Club'

The male user's reply rolled in an hour later. 'disproved by research! the three sweetest words in the english language.'

The female user replied twenty minutes after that. 'Hahahahaha. But how did we forget Jim Morrison?'

Sometimes they met outside his office and got drinks close by, other times they went to a film or a concert or an exhibition. Most times they watched shows on the male user's laptop.

The male user enjoyed their time together best when it was mediated by an object of mutual focus, when they shared in the suspension of their patterns of day-to-day thinking. It made being around one another easier to regulate; kept boredom out of the room. No pressure to act or feel a certain way.

When they spent time in each other's company raw, the male user felt ill at ease. Mornings, he felt trapped in the minutes it took the female user to leave his apartment.

The male user lay watching the ceiling with the female user three-quarters prone, head resting on the flat of his chest.

He cleared his throat and said, in a thin voice, 'When I was fifteen—'

The female user opened her eyes and waited for him to continue. She hadn't noticed herself falling asleep before. A minute passed in silence until she closed her eyes again. When she reopened them, in what felt like the minute following that, soft dawn light backlit the bedroom curtains.

'Hey! How's it going? Do you maybe want to get dinner this week? We're going to try and set a record for latest barbecue of the year if the weather holds.'

The female user reread the message and deleted: 'We're going to try and set a record for latest barbecue of the year if the weather holds.' Then she deleted: 'How's it going?' Then she also deleted: 'Do you maybe want to get dinner this week?'

After substituting '!' with '?', the female user sent the message to the male user. She had never needed to contact him in a way that felt so one-sided and inorganic before; since meeting in person, message-interactions between the two of them had always taken place in the context of an ongoing exchange of moment-to-moment observations.

So as not to spend the rest of her evening actively anticipating the male user's reply, the female user went to see a film alone. The film's central conceit was: what if an averagely attractive woman hit her head and gained the erroneous belief that she was above averagely attractive. In the film's romantic subplot, the averagely attractive woman won over a man of equally average attractiveness with her newfound confidence.

Waiting for the film to be over, the female user thought in pulses about the male user, who she worried lately had been distant, different-acting. Whereas before he'd always replied to her texts within thirty to forty minutes, he now took two to three hours to produce responses that were both less thoughtful and less interesting than the ones he'd previously taken a quarter of the time to compose. Either the male user's interest in responding to her had decreased, or he was taking an increasing amount of pleasure in making her wait for his responses.

The two users hadn't made any plans for the coming Friday evening or subsequent weekend, the leisure times they most frequently spent together. The female user fretted that, without the steady, episodic structure of their routines holding them in place, they might decelerate out of the rhythms of each other's lives completely.

Although the female user had been careful not to allow the male user to become her sole source of life's pleasure, meeting him had undeniably renewed her interest in herself. Her positive moods and feelings of self-worth were, she realised now, contingent upon the quality of the attention he gave her.

The female user left the multiplex feeling worse than she had entering it. When she next checked her smartphone, the male user had not yet responded to her message. On her bus ride home, she wondered if he still used the algorithm-based dating app.

The male user began to wonder if the algorithm-based dating app had eroded his empathy. On some level, he felt sure classifying women into bipartite categories of datable or not based solely on their physical qualities was retrograde non-feminist activity, and that using the algorithm-based dating app encouraged (if not outright rewarded) many of the worst aspects of the male gaze as he was able to comprehend it. That some inversion of the gaze was reflected back at him, that he too was a vulnerable entrant into the same pageant of which he was also a judge, felt like it somewhat diminished the problem of the gaze – but diminished it by how much, exactly?

The male user had started to see women as oddly clone-like since getting heavily into the app, as if each woman with whom he matched was a continuation of the one preceding her. (The fact that, for reasons of personal taste, most of the women he matched with *were* broadly similar only intensified this distortion in his perspective. As if to gauge the extent of their sameness, the male user had, the previous week, taken two female users to the same bar within two days of each other, and had had there almost identical interactions with them both.)

The male user considered the further flaws of the algorithm-based dating app. To experience early-stage romance easily and frequently discounts its value. By joining the algorithm-based dating app in the first place, users are, from the get-go, demonstrating the perforce failure of their romantic lives; their personal defectiveness and unlovability. Owing to the replicable means of their production, app-contrived relationships take on a modular structure, a design that fosters interchangeability. Relationships initiated by the algorithm-based dating app have no solid grounding in reality – no surrounding context – and, as such, unfold with the drifting narrative coherence of dreams.

Plus the male user worried increasingly about getting the female user pregnant, which until recently had also been his main sexual fantasy. He decided that, given the risks involved, he would probably never sleep with the female user again, and then tried not to think about her at all after that. He felt like he'd completed a phase. Maybe soon he would find a new long-term sexual partner – maybe one with tattoos.

Increasingly, the male user had become host to the thought of a boring, monastic life he knew he would probably hate. He envisioned a long abstinence from sensorial immersion. He could read more: be the guy who reads. He liked the way that sounded.

Sometimes the male user wanted to blunt every pleasure-receiving nerve he had. He thought in the obvious metaphors, and pictured a cutting of strings.

In her cubicle, the female user laid her smartphone screen-side up on the desk next to her keyboard and clicked it locked. She watched its vivid, OLED display dim to a panel of solid black.

It had been a day, a night and a morning since the female user had last messaged the male user, to which she had still not received any response. In fact, outside of a text from a franchise pizza chain advertising an online exclusive deal on garlic-and-mozzarella bread and a text requesting birthday-present ideas from her mother, the female user hadn't received any messages from anyone via any platform in three days.

Am I a loser? Have I made the right choices?

Sometimes the female user felt like everything that happened inside a device, in screen time, occurred in something like the present, while everything that happened outside of one, in real time, occurred in something like the past.

The female user sent some productive work emails and scraped back her cuticles for the duration of time it took her thoughts to return to the male user.

They had slept under the same sheet together the last four consecutive weekends. If you counted her mouth, he had come inside her upwards of fifteen times. They had in-jokes and places they liked. He had seen her in all her best clothes.

She knew, of course, that if she were the male user, she would treat herself exactly the same way he had, with the same sense of touristic irresponsibility toward a life that seemed to end at the limits of his field of vision. The algorithm would dispense to the male user a thousand other matches, each one fresh as an individually packaged spearmint. The algorithm's preferences for more and for new would shape his own.

If the male user sent her a long message tenderly explaining all the reasons why he didn't want to see her anymore, the female user wouldn't read it, but that didn't mean she wouldn't like him to send one. Was he planning on just avoiding her? For the rest of his life? The more she thought about it, the angrier she got.

On her smartphone, the female user navigated back to her messaging-app conversation with the male user where her 'Hey?' still hovered pathetically between them, sealed in the azure-blue of its speech-bubble vector.

'So', she typed in the text box beneath it and deleted. 'Why', she typed and deleted. She glanced at the messaging app's predictive-text function, which she mostly only ever ignored. She moved her thumb toward one of the three words it had preselected for her based on her historical word choices.

'Yeah', she selected. A new assortment of predictive follow-up words appeared onscreen. She hesitated, then chose: 'I'm sure it's going on a couple of days more but I'm very sure it is just what you could do I gotta get you some stuff out there I know I like you and sorry you know how much you're having fun I didn't want to have to do anything sorry actually', return, return, return, send.

Excuse Me, Don't I Know You?

That was what he'd said.

She spun around thinking, from the sound of his voice, *Surely it's not*—, her surroundings revolving and blurring together, *There's no way it's*— Then all things refilled their outlines, and there he clearly was.

They were standing, several persons apart, in line for a stall at a biweekly farmer's market hosted on the forecourt of a church close to where she lived: she, wearing her backpack around frontways; he, encumbered with a large houseplant. Above them both, the overcast midday sky was the colour of the *Financial Times*.

'Oh, hi,' she said. Was she smiling just because it was nice to be recognised, or was she smiling because it was, specifically, him? 'I'm buying some vegetables' was all she could think to say next, then chinned, downwardly, toward her backpack.

Passers-by were moving awkwardly around and joining the queue behind him; he took a few sidesteps and tilted his head in the direction of a less busy area of the market. '*I'll wait over there*,' he mouthed, exaggeratedly.

Realising now that Nick was not actually an occupant

of the same queue as she was, Julia nodded at him, also exaggeratedly.

After she'd paid for her produce and manoeuvred her backpack back around normalways, she walked slowly over toward him – aware of the reinforcement but not the reality of the ground beneath her feet. That she had encountered him here, in situ, out of the context of the past, was taking her some serious mental processing power to compute.

They semicircled one another with half-hugs, both mentioning how surprised they felt – wasn't life funny that way.

'I have to say,' Nick said, 'I'm really impressed with myself. I could tell from all the way over there' – he gestured behind him – 'that you were you, based solely on the back of your head.'

Julia's hand rose, involuntarily, to touch her hair. 'I'll take it as a compliment.'

Dispositionally averse to having meaningful conversations while standing still, Nick said, 'So, what's going on'; asked, 'D'you maybe want to go for a walk?'

Julia said sure, that sounded great.

They exited the consecrated grounds together through the lychgate, uncommon out here in the city.

'Well,' Nick said, cross-examining Julia as she cross-examined him in return; each one also simultaneously imagining themselves from the other's point of view, 'how are you? You look—'

'I'm good.'

'You look good.'

'Thanks.'

'Which way're we heading?'

The regular coordinates of Julia's sense of direction had been momentarily scrambled; she paused to get her bearings. 'Thataway.'

'Cool.' Nick transferred the weight of the houseplant across sides of his body, introducing support from one thigh as he did so, holding it now under his opposite arm.

'This is so crazy,' Julia said. 'What's a guy like you doing all the way out here?'

Nick shrugged as best he could while still holding the plant, 'I live near here.'

'You do?'

'Yeah. Like, fifteen minutes' walk.'

'So *crazy*,' she repeated, although she guessed it wasn't really that crazy; most people she knew seemed to live in this part of the city at some point in their lives. 'And, so, for how long have you lived around here?'

'A year or something?'

Julia, noting inwardly that Nick was a slow walker: 'You're kidding.'

'Yeah,' he said, 'I mean, no, I'm not. I knew you were

around here too. I would've said hi or something, but—'

'*But?*'

'Well, I heard you weren't seeing much of Roos or Teddy anymore, so I didn't want to' – he looked at Julia, then past her – 'I don't know. Cramp your style.'

'Cramp my style?'

'It's just that Teddy said you were going out with a restaurateur or something, and—'

'A head chef, not a—'

'Right, right. Right. Right, but, still, it sounded like you had a new friend line-up going on. Was all I thought.'

'I still see Teddy,' Julia said, defensively, before remembering it'd been almost six months since the time they'd gotten coffee, 'sometimes.'

It was true she'd fallen out of the social orbit of her old friendship circle, and she wished now she had a better excuse for why that'd happened other than 'work'. But she *had* been working really hard lately – sometimes she put in sixty-hour weeks at the kitchen.

Still, it was sad to think of all the old friends she lived so close to and never saw; their lives going on in parallel, untouching.

Nick mistook Julia's last few seconds of silence for an open invitation to probe further into her love life. 'So how's that working out, anyway?'

'How's what working out?'

170

'With the old guy? I mean, the guy. The chef.'

They were passing through an area of the city that had been notoriously gentrified ten or twenty years before, and which currently seemed to be in the process of being re- or hyper-gentrified – tenement buildings razed to make way for luxury apartments; boutique stores evicted to accommodate chains.

Here, Julia found herself caught between two competing, equal-strength conversation-with-an-ex impulses: to be her honest self and reveal her life for the capsizing mess it was, or to lie and sustain an image of being put-together; everything going great. 'Everything's going great.'

'Oh yeah?'

'Yeah.' Then, to tell enough of a version of the truth so as not to feel fully like a liar: 'I mean, we *have* taken a temporary break to see how things go. Just for now. We're very different people.'

'Yeah?'

'Yeah. Like, almost as different as it's possible for two people to be. Temperamentally. Life-experience-ally.'

'I see. You were classically trained at Juilliard, and he learned to dance out on the streets.'

'Actually, that's kind of almost accurate. And I did do ballet classes when I was a kid.'

'I remember,' Nick said, 'I've seen your feet.'

Every quarter-kilometre or so, branches of the same

few banks, convenience supermarkets, coffee chains and betting shops repeated themselves, like in the background of an old cartoon. Lately, Nick had been wondering who the city was for.

'How d'you mean?'

'As in, it's clearly not intended for you or me. All these luxury high-rises only get constructed to silo the wealth of, like, foreign investors.'

Julia thought it sounded like Nick was trying out recently acquired knowledge. Then, sure enough:

'I just read an article about how more than half of all the new new-builds built in the city last year are sitting empty now. Because they're not really designed for people, just as holdings for—'

Nick stopped at a zebra crossing and Julia pushed, lightly, on the small of his back to get him to keep walking. 'It's our right of way.'

'Sure,' he said, watchful of an approaching Audi that was slow to slow down as they crossed. 'Anyway, I'll send you the article. But, my point is, I'm very much looking forward to moving out of here soon.'

Julia wagged a forefinger, sang: 'Everyone says they want to leave, but no one ever does.'

'Oh, no, I actually am leaving.'

'When?'

'At the end of the month.'

'You are?' Julia said, quickly dissembling the expression of genuine surprise that had taken hold of her face. 'I'm shocked.'

'Ten minutes ago you didn't even know I was here.'

'But now I'm *shocked*.' At the risk of coming across as having become actually upset, Julia decided to retrofit her initial reaction into a meta-level joke about how laughable the idea of her becoming upset was. '*Affronted*, even. *Beside* myself. *Sobbing*, practically. Whereabouts are you going?'

Nick inhaled in preparation to say something he knew was deeply lame. 'I'm moving back in with my parents.'

Not knowing how to respond to this – but also knowing she only had a limited time in which to non-awkwardly issue her response – Julia said, 'Oh?' like a character in a historical romance novel.

With his free hand, Nick rubbed his nose. 'At least for a little while.'

'What's the thinking there?'

'Well, I have some things to sort out. My entire life, for one.'

'That's— I admire—' Julia searched around for something to find admirable about Nick's situation, '—your courage.'

'My courage?' He looked annoyed. 'So, I'm courageous for moving back in with my parents after failing to build a life for myself away from them?'

Obviously I was only trying to be nice, Julia thought. 'Exactly,' she said.

The streets were getting narrower and busier; they both struggled to prioritise between multiple attention-worthy external stimuli.

'This way?' Julia pointed in the direction of a residential side road.

Nick said sure, and together they exited the centre of the gentrificationscape; the buildings surrounding them becoming gradually more dilapidated.

'And, what about your job?'

Nick readjusted the position of the potted palm he was carrying, so now all its weight rested on his hip, like a baby. 'What about my job?'

'Are you going to quit? When you move back home?'

'Wasn't planning on it, no. I'll commute. It's only, like, an hour and a half's travel' – he winced as he mentally mapped out the journey – 'each way.'

Julia remembered how hopeless Nick had been with planning and organisation back at university; the way he'd floundered around post-graduation without any real aim or ambition. His lack of direction had been a deciding factor for her in choosing to break up with him.

Trying to make the question sound unloaded, she asked: 'And what is it you do for work now?'

'Copywriting. At a marketing firm. But it's barely even a job. I just sit in front of a computer all day and sometimes get told what to type.'

'That sounds interesting,' she said, hopefully.

'It isn't,' he said. With every downstep he took, the houseplant's outermost fronds tapped annoyingly against the side of his face. 'I'll apply for other jobs soon, though; figure things out. The city isn't the be-all and end-all. Then, from there, who knows.'

'And are you still doing your own writing? Like, "writing" writing?'

'Trying to, sure, always,' Nick said, embarrassed, thinking about all the recent stories, draft screenplays and novels-in-progress he'd started and abandoned, unable to make them effortlessly cohere like the juvenilia he'd written at university.

They transitioned into a quieter street with fewer points of access to commercial goods and services.

'So, d'you still love living here?' he said, steering the conversation deliberately away from the subject of his writing.

'Me? I do love it, yeah,' she said, reflexively, then paddled little circles in the air with her hands; 'I mean, but, I also feel kind of negative about it, sometimes.

'As in, the longer I stay,' she went on, after a brief pause, 'the more I feel like I'm being warped into the mould of a city-person. Being ground down. Which sort of makes me feel hopeless and doomed.'

Nick nodded. 'So, what's keeping you here?'

Good question.

To which the obvious answer was: where else could she go? All her friends were here, even though she never saw them, and so was her job, even though she didn't like it. This was, supposedly, the city where opportunity ran thick and fun things happened. There was no real alternative, and that alone had to justify its crippling cost of living and almost-unbreathable air.

If she was being honest, for every one thing she loved about the city, she could think of a hundred others she was coming to loathe about it. Briefly, she rethought her entire adult life.

'I don't know,' she said, then laughed. 'This is turning into a high-intensity conversation.'

'True, sorry,' Nick said, renegotiating his bodily equilibrium with relation to the houseplant.

In an area containing more affordable rental properties, they passed tens of mid-twenties-aged couples, which, for a weird moment, made Julia feel subconsciously like she and Nick were also a couple themselves.

She blinked fast a few times, trying to reroute her thoughts. 'Hey, so, what's with the big plant?' she said, to say something.

176

'What?'

'Like, why'd you buy a big plant when you're moving away so soon?'

'Nothing gets past you, does it, Detective? It's for your old friend Roos.'

Julia swallowed, but the question still came out drily: 'Why?'

'Well, we've been seeing a lot more of each other lately' – Nick shook the plant by the pot, rustling its fan-like leaves – 'so I wanted to get her a kind of goodbye present.'

Nick waited for Julia to respond somehow, but she didn't.

'You should call her sometime. We could all hang out.'

'I know I should,' Julia said. What, exactly, was she hearing here, and why did she feel so blindsided by it? Were her ex and her ex-best friend—?

'She's dating this really nice guy now,' Nick said, 'Stanislaw. D'you remember him?'

'Maybe,' she said, feeling instant low-level relief. 'From third year?'

A bus overtook a cyclist on the road beside them; Nick said something Julia failed to properly hear over the sound of the vehicle's acceleration. She nodded and said, 'For sure' anyway.

Talking about Roos had set her thinking about certain decisions she'd made over the last few years, none of which had seemed particularly significant at the time, but which had all transformed her – incrementally, across days – into a withdrawn, work-oriented person who no longer had many friends. She wondered if she'd changed too much, now, to recommence those old friendships.

As an experiment, she looked at Nick and tried to pull an in-joke from their shared cache of private references; years of interpersonal experiences that only they had in common. Not a single thing came to mind.

A light rain had begun to fall, invisible in mid-air but manifesting as a constellation of discoloured discs out on the road and pavement.

It was nice to be here with Julia, Nick thought – a reassurance, in many ways – to exist again alongside her. The warm, barely noticeable rain brought the moment into a kind of thematic continuity with other important moments he'd experienced amid rains over the course of his life. Someday he would write them all down.

Then he started talking at her about the earth's finite reserves of extractable petroleum. 'D'you remember how, back at university, everyone was worried about "peak oil"?' Lately, Nick had gotten into a bad habit of looking off into the middle distance as he recited long passages of information he'd memorised from online; he indulged that habit now. 'There were always protests and debates on campus about how there's only a limited quantity of recoverable oil left beneath the earth's surface, and that pretty soon geological scarcity would start imposing hard limits on economic and production-related growth – as in, mass-inflating commodity prices; intensifying proxy and resource wars; and, eventually, collapsing the global economy. *But*, have you noticed that, nowadays, you basically never hear the term "peak oil" anymore? Which is weird because, if you look it up, forecasters say we're edging still closer to peak oil year on year – as in, it's only, like, one or two decades away from actually happening now. *Apparently*, that's because there was all this research published a few years ago saying not to worry about peak oil because it was only a hoax, but *then* it turned out that *that* research was all oil-industry-funded, to soothe the market or whatever. It's interesting, right? Like, it's weird how—' He quarter-turned to gauge Julia's response to what he'd been saying, realised she was no longer beside him, then quarter-turned again to find she'd stopped walking several full sentences of his monologue ago.

'Sorry Nick,' she said, operating her smartphone; tiny raindrops bejewelling its screen. She looked up: 'I am listening, I just need to text someone. One second.' She looked back down at her smartphone and saw that, weirdly, she'd also managed to type the thing she'd only meant to say: *Sorry Nick*.

Although he secretly felt Julia's withdrawal of her smartphone had broken the spell of their run-in's serendipity, Nick said no worries.

Julia could sense him studying her face as she deleted and typed more words; she told him to look in another direction, and he did.

'Are you texting a *boy*?' Nick said, uptalking the word 'boy' at the last moment to backload the question with jokey intonation.

'No,' Julia said, 'not that it's any of your business,' in a way that, Nick felt, successfully simultaneously chided both his nosiness and tendency toward narrow-minded, regressively heteronormative thinking. He briefly imagined Julia starring in a high-production-value TV miniseries, navigating well-lit, cosmopolitan romantic relationships with persons of all genders.

'Why are you nodding?' Julia said, depositing her smartphone into her backpack's front pocket and zipping it shut.

'I wasn't.'

'Yes you were. And if you must know' – she started them both walking again – 'I was texting my sister.'

At the same time that Nick said, 'How's she doing?' Julia said, 'I think she's got pre-getting-married nerves.'

'No way. I didn't even know she was engaged. Well, I guess why would I. To that solicitor guy?'

180

'Yeah. Oh no, wait. To a different solicitor guy than the one you're thinking of.'

'How history repeats—'

'And here's another thing you don't know: she's pregnant. And she and her fiancé are moving to Toronto.'

'Toronto, *Canada*?' Nick said, pointlessly.

'Correct. Her *hus*-band's firm is giving him a big pro-*mo*-tion.'

'Wow. And will you go out to visit them?'

'I mean, it's far,' Julia said, 'and expensive. But I definitely will. I want to, as soon as I can. After the baby's born.' She bit the inside of her cheek; time really was just vanishing. 'But anyway, yeah, peak oil. I think I vaguely remember being outraged about it at some point.'

At the corner of the park Julia used to cross every day on her walk to her old job, Nick asked if they could shelter for a minute under a tree – his arms needed a rest from carrying the plant. Julia said sure.

He lit, then seconds later relit, a hand-rolled cigarette she hadn't even noticed him producing. He offered her a drag, which she declined.

The rain continued falling faintly all around them. For a while, they discussed the postgraduate lives of people they'd known at university; a former mutual friend who, over the past year, had taken up what essentially amounted to a full-time, unpaid position as a microfamous public scold on social media. At some point, Julia reported to Nick the likely consequences that the deregulated sale of chlorinated chicken would have on the restaurant industry at large.

The more they talked, the less Nick could think to say. Was it just him, or did it feel like there was some vast, elephantoid, unspoken issue between them that they were failing to acknowledge? But what? Time's relentless flow? World events? The fact that, once, they'd made each other truly happy?

Nick shivered and outheld an upturned palm from under the tree's cover to monitor the rain. 'Hey, so, I'm going over there.' He pointed off in the direction of a neighbourhood Julia didn't know so well.

'Alright,' she said. For a single, specially designated moment, she allowed herself to feel disappointed.

'This is kind of my new thing,' he said, 'leaving at the opportune time. But yeah. I'll email you that article?'

'That'd be nice.'

'And d'you still have the same email?'

'Yeah,' Julia said, warmly, but thinking: *Who changes their email?* 'And send me some of your stories. If you're still writing them.'

'Cool,' he said, embarrassed again at the mention of his writing. He removed a stray fibre of tobacco particulate from his bottom lip. 'Well, truly good to see you.'

She smiled, and non-seriously considered doing some-thing insane – screaming with abandon, punching him, making a move – just to reality-test his reaction. 'Likewise.'

'Alright,' he said; shook his head; ventured a look at her face. 'Small world. Or, no, it's just around here that's small. But still.'

They hugged, said goodbye, then left each other alone.

Knowing she shouldn't, she turned around and watched him walk away. Only from a distance did she realise they were both wearing the exact same model of low-top, unisex vegan shoe in differing colourways. She consid-ered maybe texting him to point out the coincidence, but didn't. Her turning around had had its anticipated effect – she felt sadder now than she had before.

Gradually, they were both reassimilated into the same metropolis in two separate directions; whatever versions of whatever similar thoughts they were each having about their encounter reverberating in their heads.

She walked much faster on her own, and eventually realised she'd walked a ways without thinking about where she was going, then course-corrected her direc-tion toward home. She'd underslept the previous night, which was maybe why she felt so weird and feeble-mind-ed now.

Two years since she'd last seen Nick. Wait, no, she'd miscounted – three. He looked a lot better than before;

she wondered if he'd quit drinking altogether, or maybe just cut down.

Sad for him to be moving back in with his parents, but she guessed he couldn't help it. Maybe it would give him the motivation he needed to finally figure himself out.

She felt glad to have run into him, but gladder still to be alone again, back once more in the clear. It had been exhausting, keeping up the front of the girl who did everything right.

Stepping over a nacreous-coloured puddle that'd pooled in a dip in the pavement, she thought about how you had to be careful with the way you remembered things: not to allow yourself to fall into easy revisionism; not to forget romantic notions of the past were almost always fictions.

A new wind strengthened the rainfall's downward force. Cold now; she yanked hard on the hoodstrings of Ellery's old sweatshirt, toggling its neckline tighter around her neck – how quickly the weather turned unseasonable.

Did people even talk about the weather in terms of seasonability anymore? Were seasons still designated the way they used to be; did the old signifiers still apply?

Also: are coincidences messages from God? Julia knew it sounded crazy – she wasn't even really a believer – but she was raised in faith and knew exactly what her mother would say: *It's a sign.*

Surely a self-serving fallacy, though. What seemed like synchronicities were just random affordances of chance or mischance; felicities of the void.

But then. The chaos, the suffering – in a strange way, at certain hours of the day and in certain moods, it all made its own kind of perfect sense. *To desire the help of grace is the beginning of grace.* Thoughts such as these delivered her into the long evening ahead.

Search Engine Optimisation

Six white males between the ages of twenty-seven and fifty-five are seated in a room. Their Friday late-morning conference call is over, but it is too early to be reasonably lunch.

In front of each male – on the laminate, anti-fingerprint surface of the room's central table – is a photocopied, spiral-bound copy of the same presentation as is currently being overhead-projected from one of the six's laptops onto a matte canvas screen affixed to the narrower and window-less of the room's two load-bearing walls. (The room's two non-load-bearing walls are frosted-glass internal par-titions, through which only the males' beclouded outlines are visible to the rest of the office.)

The males – ranked, here, ascendingly by value of height – are: 5. Perry Avery; 4. Sean Townsend; 3. Fred Honey and Ray Bannon (tied); 2. Matt Maynard; and 1. Chris Newland.

Sean Townsend, ordinarily the first teammate to en-liven a post-meeting silence, dedicates the entirety of his executive function toward fabricating something funny to say.

189

Chris Newland sneezes thrice in quick succession; Matt Maynard blesses him once.

Ray Bannon – who today wears a tongue-coloured chambray shirt that Perry Avery cannot quite keep his eyes off – says to no one in particular, 'Did you hear today's Ontkean's last day?'

Although he seldom thinks about Henry Ontkean, for Fred Honey, the act of resignation confers a kind of heroism onto the resignee; he finds himself admiring Ontkean for getting out of here. 'Good for him. Did we hire a replacement yet?'

'Some woman, but she withdrew her application already,' Maynard says. 'Had an issue, familyside.'

Townsend's mind releases a joke: 'Ontkean's leaving? Big shoes to fill.'

Five of the males, including Townsend himself, laugh at this witticism. Honey, the lone unlaugher, wears a problem-solving face.

Bannon goes: 'He certainly has a *large* personality.'

Townsend leans back, tipping his black plastic chair onto its hind legs. 'You could say he'll leave a *jumbo-sized* dent in the—'

'Where's he headed?' Honey says.

'Ontkean?' Maynard says. 'Hasn't said. Well, haven't asked.'

Newland fingers the access lanyard that hangs about

his neck; every new starter in the building gets one, but no one else actually wears theirs. 'I think I heard' – he looks around the room for a second before failing to articulate the following straight-facedly – 'he got headhunted for a tasting job at the M&M's store.'

More group laughter. (In a far corner of the room stands a tall, maybe perennial indoor plant; hard to say, from this distance, whether it's fake or real – Honey cannot recall, with any certainty, ever having seen it being watered; he's attended Friday-morning meetings for two years now and is unsure if the plant has grown at all in that time.) 'Alright,' Honey says, 'c'mon,' and the laughs peter out.

'Ontkean's been here eleven years,' Bannon says.

Maynard echoes, 'Eleven years'; shakes his head.

Avery says, 'I joined here eight years ago. I was twenty-five. Wasn't married. Didn't have kids.'

Four of the six males who aren't Honey or Townsend bite the insides of their cheeks/lips and/or nod sagely. Each of these four meditates briefly on the sailing by of time; pictures the face of a different woman.

Townsend – who landed this job out of nepotism and has never worked anywhere else – has another funny thought. He addresses Avery specifically but plays to the room at large: 'You started here eight years ago and you've been trying to leave for seven.'

More five-headed laughter, then a recap of open issues and executable actions, outcomes from today's call; most urgently, amendments must be made to Avery's presentation deck before it gets sent to the client.

Bannon and Maynard segue into their weekly-recurrent duologue about the possibility of streamlining the firm's approach to project sign-off, which always bottlenecks where senior creative is involved. As this discussion draws out, Townsend yawns and – seeing him yawn – Honey yawns.

Signalling that the meeting is finally adjourned, Avery stands and circles the table, collecting together the presentation printouts he laid out earlier; *the colour of that shirt, my god*, he thinks, as he passes Bannon by.

Newland rises and says something about there being Danishes in the break area, then the rest of the males rise. The sextet leaves the room and soon disbands.

In a blank, unsealed, C4-sized envelope, Henry Ontkean's A4-sized novelty leaving card has been placed on Fred Honey's desk for him to sign.

The card is printed on non-premium stock paper and features, on its front, a typographic design that contains multiple swears and also the word 'Henry' – probably it was artworked internally.

Honey opens the card and skims the messages already handwritten therein: 'You'll be missed'; 'All best for the future'; 'A pleasure working with you.'

Honey uncaps a ballpoint pen and writes 'Keep in touch' in an empty corner of the card, followed by his initials. Written down – and surrounded by so much free space – the message reads as excessively formal, soulless.

He considers drawing a smiley face after the word 'touch', but doesn't. He reinserts the card into the envelope, which he deposits on Chloe Daley's desk.

'What's the meaning of this?' Chloe Daley says, smiling toward the end of her sentence.

'Just a love letter, Chloe,' Fred Honey says, standing over her as she sits.

'*Finally*.'

Honey picks up and revolutes a few times the promotional, conference-branded fidget spinner Daley keeps on her desk. 'What're you doing?'

'Working,' Daley says.

'Are you distractible?'

'Kind of busy.'

'Lunch soon?'

For non-executive staff, Friday means dress-down; Daley wears a pre-faded maroon graphic tee with a

193

generic surf-related slogan screen-printed on it. 'Yeah, but probably right here,' she says, an index finger referring downwardly to her workstation.

'Smoking today?'

'Mabes,' she says, 'I'm down to, like, five a week.'

'Well,' Honey says, setting the spinner down as its weighted lobes lose momentum and cease blurring together, 'come grab me if you're still addicted after lunch.'

Because she is so pretty, Chloe Daley has the power to enter people's dreams.

Fred Honey selects the last remaining cherry-jam Danish from an opened carton of Costco pastries, its cellophane veil now completely shed. A Post-it affixed to the wall behind the carton reads: 'My treat, enjoy. – Henry.'

The Danish has staled in the air-conditioned air. Eating it, Honey settles into a preferred fantasy of his last day here. He will bring in a Krispy Kreme premium non-ring dozen with personalised raspberry-glaze lettering that reads 'FUCK YOU ALL' across the individual doughnuts – twelve exact characters including spaces.

Several feet away from him, a sleepy-looking Nick Dwyer is reheating leftovers in the break area microwave.

'Hi Nick,' Honey says, around a mouthful of pastry shards. 'Weekend plans?'

Dwyer has not spoken for so long today his lips have stuck together. After a second: 'I think I'm just— Yeah. I have some stuff— Going on. How about you?' The microwave knells; from it, Dwyer removes an unlidded Tupperware containing a cuboid, cross-sectional slice of lasagne.

'This and that,' Honey says. 'Have you signed Henry's leaving card?'

'No, but I will,' Dwyer says, 'forthwith,' awkward and tryhard; the way he talks embarrasses them both. 'Well.' He holds up and shakes his lunch – which he always eats early and alone – and says, in this painstakingly cheerful way, 'Have a good one, Fred.'

For the first time in human history, no person has to think their own thoughts if they don't want to. Technology has opened new slots in the world through which instant, sub-stanceless, distractive relief is accessible to the consumer at any moment.

Anyone you talk to is simultaneously half-present in a more entertaining, disembodied social space that exists in an onscreen tangent-reality. Meanwhile, interactions that occur between persons in physical, non-virtual space feel increasingly overburdened with a diffuse anxiety directly counter-related to the highly optimised ease of use of tech-mediated communication.

The more we interact across screens, the rarer and less bearable our face-to-face interactions are becoming. Or, at least, that's how Nick Dwyer feels.

Kate Batchelder shuffles together a loose sheaf of papers on her desk; like a newscaster, knocks them into an even-sided stack. *That's that*, she thinks, definitive, all her morning's tasks completed, *that's that*.

She thinks it again several more times as she carries the papers over to the paper shredder; enjoys the looping, ouroboric logic of the phrase: *That's that that's that that's that*.

Already operating the shredder when she reaches the print room is Chris Newland.

'Hey Chris,' Batchelder says, which goes unheard beneath the shredder's industrial whirring. She feels like she's standing too close behind him, so retreats enough backsteps to where she's leaning up against a wall.

Newland's deep focus on the act of inserting paper into the shredder's maw has relaxed all the muscles in his face. After he finishes feeding in one document, he withdraws another from a ring-bound binder labelled 'SHREDDA-BLE' and loads it into the machine.

He flinches hard when, eventually, he becomes aware of Batchelder's presence. 'Jesus. Sorry, Kate. Didn't see you there. Be one minute.'

'Take your time,' Batchelder says.

But Newland being Newland, he starts rushing and, within moments, he's overloaded the shredder by forcing a too-thick batch of papers into its entry port. On the shredder's frontal console, an LED that usually glows solid green now starts blinking red.

'Hell on earth,' Newland says to himself; the formerly relaxed muscles of his face all tightening. He attempts to manually unjam the wad of papers, but the shredder is uncooperative. 'So. Impractical,' he says – long pause between the words.

It takes Batchelder a second to think to offer to do something. 'Should I go fetch Gigi from downstairs?'

Newland grunts bisyllabically ('Nnn-mmm'), his face magenta-ing as he wrangles with the stuck sheets of paper, some of which tear apart in his hands.

Batchelder knows better than to offer reasonable advice to someone who is still in the commencement phase of getting annoyed. Even so, she says: 'Let me quickly run and get Gigi, he can always—'

'I *know* I can fix this,' Newland says, his voice shading hostile, 'I just can't do it with you standing there watching me.'

197

Ray Bannon has upbuilt his post-divorce self-confidence through a regimen of high-intensity interval training, sensible eating and measured participation in online fora dedicated to pick-up-artistry and men's rights activism.

A useful thing Bannon has learned from the manosphere is to remember one personal fact about each of his co-workers, and then to make casual reference to that fact when engaged with them in conversation. By doing this, he hopes to be perceived as likeable and charismatic. For instance: Chloe Daley is training for a half-marathon; Leanne Kelly has an infant son; Fred Honey recently went through a bad break-up.

Sean Townsend passes Gigi Parras in the hallway, says a swift: 'Heya, Gi.'

Parras says a heya back, but does not look at Townsend.

Gigi Parras's office reputation is he's a stickler, plays with a straight bat.

Attends, but does not drink at, Thursday after-work beers. Is unmarried and of indeterminate age. Does not participate in the weekly officewide lottery syndicate. On weekends, has been sighted wearing the exact same smart-casual kinds of clothing as he wears Monday through Friday. When talked about in groups that exclude him, is criticised only, if at all, for coming across as aloof.

Although the office is definitely dated, it is impossible to isolate exactly which era the office is dated from.

Leanne Kelly distinctly remembers hearing someone once mention that Pullman, Townsend & Pyatt's head-quarters were established here in 2002, but the building itself is clearly way older than that – like mid-seventies to early eighties.

Funny how none of the executive staff understands that it is easier to pass the time in a pleasanter room. As in, why make us all sit here under fluorescent striplights, yel-lowing drop ceilings; why make us endure crowded desk space, never-changed potpourri – even just some minor renovations would make a big difference. It's like, can't we have anything nice?

'Can I just say something, though,' Perry Avery says.

Several of them are standing in the break area debating a politics-adjacent issue that has dominated mainstream news coverage now for weeks. What began as a loose, current-affairs-based conversation between two people has overrun into an argument spanning five raised voices.

'Can I just say,' Perry Avery repeats, and then goes on to also repeat, verbatim, a point he heard on talk radio a few drivetimes ago.

After Avery finishes, Sam Wendt raises a counterpoint, with which two of the four other persons in the break area also vocally agree.

The foremost agreer is Chloe Daley, who proceeds to speak informedly and passionately about the issue at hand, although – sobering thought – the more she talks, the harder it becomes for her to actually tell if she even really cares about the issue, or if she's just reciting a series of prefabricated talking points that've been fed to her via a giant cross-media broadcasting apparatus. If the former, why doesn't she care more? If the latter, what're all these thoughts doing in her head?

Now Chris Newland speaks up in defence of Perry Avery. (As Newland's eyes meet Daley's, he experiences a flashback to a recent dream in which he nursed, baby-like, at her breast; the dream-image rises momentarily in his mind before, just as quickly, he suppresses it.)

Wendt then rounds on Newland, then Newland responds to Wendt and Daley. As he does so, Daley notices a good amount of plaque deposited along the gumline of Newland's bottom row of teeth. Not wanting to look at the rest of him, she stares down at his shoes as she offers her rebuttal. Again, while she talks, the same strange feeling as before. Something impersonal about everything she's saying; someone else's words she's using.

Still, Ray Bannon – arms folded, nodding – seems to agree with all Daley's opinions about the politics-adjacent issue; makes these little humming noises of affirmation.

Daley's getting involved in this conversation was wholly self-inflicted. She never should've asked Avery and Bannon what they were talking about; she only came to the break area to make coffee.

See how Newland, who's talking now, clamps his eyelids shut every time he blinks. It's a nerves thing that's impossible to un-notice after you've noticed it – a tic that worsens in Daley's presence, like he's winking at her with both eyes.

Out of the goodness of her heart, Daley listens to Newland; lets him explain back to her a bunch of things she basically already knows.

Then Wendt interrupts Newland and, while all the men are arguing, Daley quietly exits the break area. Only when she arrives back at her desk does she realise she forgot to make the coffee she went over there to make in the first place.

Yesterday, Gigi Parras stayed behind after hours to leave an anonymous note in the top drawer of Sean Townsend's underdesk bureau.

After Parras printed out the carefully worded note and psyched himself up to deliver it – having triple-checked to ensure the building's custodians had finished performing their final daily clean-up – he crept, semi-crouched (note folded into four; stowed in his shirt pocket), across the deserted office floor.

Deep intake of breath as he knelt by the bureau; with one smooth gesture, he slid open its top drawer, where a few bunched-up Kleenexes, which Parras momentarily mistook for the cut heads of white roses, rolled down slowly as if to greet him.

As the Kleenexes morphed, in Parras's perspective, from the clustered petals of perennial flowers into their real, three-ply tissue-paper forms, he slammed the drawer shut in disgust; stood up, awash with sudden horror, and paced multiple circuits of the empty office (note still folded in shirt pocket), hands on his hips the whole time.

Kate Batchelder has learned, in the course of her life and career, to tolerate discomfort by strategically distracting herself from it. For instance: she listens to podcasts while she does data entry to separate herself from the task.

Passing by the break area, Ray Bannon double-nods and says, 'Ladies,' to Chloe Daley and Leanne Kelly, who – once he's out of earshot – commence mocking his calculated, impersonal friendliness; how, in conversation, he manages to strike this totally unique balance of being both somehow coldly transactional and also weirdly personal. 'It's like he's talking to himself in a mirror when he talks to you,' Daley says, 'like he's *practising*.'

'He always asks me about my son,' Kelly says. 'It's creepy.'

'And the aftershave he wears' – Daley checks over her shoulder, making sure he's definitely gone – 'even when he leaves a room, he's still basically there. It's like there's a perfume ghost that haunts wherever he's been.'

All that, combined with his embarrassing, croupier-style fashion sense of waistcoats and pomade, Kelly says: 'It makes you feel sad to talk to him.'

In his capacity as acting IT engineer, Gigi Parras has obtained back-end access to the keystroke-logging employee-surveillance software installed on every desk- and laptop in the office.

In principle, this software allows Parras to gather

anonymised, unbiased datasets to generate employee engagement and cyberthreat-detection insights for the overall dual companywide benefits of (1) improving operational efficiency and (2) strengthening information security. In practice, Parras uses this software to snoop on the digital private lives of his colleagues.

Via the software's management-side interface, Parras can, in real time, monitor all the small data his co-workers enter into their computers: every message they send; every note they take; every question they ask of a search engine. To have access to all this information, Parras thinks, is to be as good as omniscient in the modern age.

Nothing in the software's TOS, nor in the company's privacy policy, explicitly forbids Parras from running his own personal digital panopticon per se, although he does so in total secrecy, well aware that he's, in bad faith, exploiting a loophole that's contingent upon a rare alignment of multiple open windows of opportunity which all have to do with PT&P's recent corporate restructuring and subsequent mismanagement of its internal resources – the only thing he's really violating, in other words, is his co-workers' trust, which isn't, technically, a fireable offence.

Nick Dwyer can barely make his eyes go across the screen to read the paragraph of text he's copyediting for Perry

Avery. Summoning his entire effort of will, he still cannot muster the readerly strength required to process the sentences currently open on his laptop without taking a break between each word to reflect on how much of a chore this simple task is proving to be.

The sub-two-hundred words of text Dwyer has to edit are intended to preface a presentation deck scheduled for internal sign-off and client delivery by close of play this afternoon. Realistically, there are at most thirty minutes of actual work here for Dwyer to complete, although the task will take him somewhere in excess of three hours to fulfil – or that, at least, is how long he'll log the task as having taken him to fulfil when, later, he updates his daily timesheet.

Small projects like these depend upon a level of inefficiency to turn a profit: the bureaucratic business model of the creative industry is to strategically over-allocate professional resources; the opposite of labour-saving. The more billable time you can expend on a project, the more money the company can justifiably charge to its client. The best work ethic you can have around here is a bad one.

Dwyer highlights and unhighlights a field of electronic text; makes some minor grammatical amendments: flips a few sentences from passive to active voice; dumbs down some smart words, smartens up some dumb words.

Honestly, though, you could replace this whole thing with lorem ipsum and no one would even notice the difference; clients only look at headings and graphics anyway.

The insertion-point text cursor blinks, expectant, on the document's open page. Dwyer's mousepad with memory-foam wrist support itches where his skin abuts the cushioning.

He forces his eyes to scan another sentence left to right, releasing a small mammalian whimper as he does so – every additional word he reads extracts something vital from him.

His mind wanders and, reflexively, he launches his web browser; clocks back into a trance-like, internet-induced state of sensory dislocation; forgets all about his wrist on the ergonomic mousepad.

He opens a pair of new tabs in which to commence work on his two main personal side projects; when absorbed in either one of them – be it his long emails to Julia or the short stories he secretly composes from his desk – the hours pass smoothly and full of meaning.

Only not so secret, the stories – nor, for that matter, the emails to Julia – given that every keystroke and mouse-click Nick Dwyer inputs into his company laptop is real-time tracked by Gigi Parras.

Right now, it looks to Parras like Dwyer is rewriting the ending of one of his stories in between moments of light copyediting in an almost-due presentation file.

It is, of course, incredibly embarrassing to have someone see you futzing around on the web, but it is also secondhand-embarrassing to bear witness to another's futzing. But as much as Parras is ashamed of his spying, he simply cannot look away.

His direct-dial extension rings; he answers; it's Chloe Daley raising a ticket. Whenever she opens a new tab in her browser, it loads up a website called 'about:blank'. What should she do about that?

'That's normal,' Parras says.

'Are you sure? It seems pretty abnormal to me.'

'You can change your homepage settings using your browser's toolbar.' A pause. 'Or the Preferences menu.' Another pause. 'I can come up and show you in five minutes?'

'Could you?'

It's always something here. Perry Avery can never connect to a printer. The meeting room's Wi-Fi speeds are too slow. Last week, a phishing email circulated around the office that took the form of a warning about a phishing email circulating around the office.

Parras checks for any interesting recent activity on Daley's laptop; via his live key-log readout, sees she's spent the last fifteen minutes search-engining the 'about:blank' issue.

Meanwhile, Leanne Kelly looks up a celebrity's height, then converts that resultant height's unit of measurement from metres into feet and inches.

Caroline Rochefort is browsing project director interviewee candidates on an integrated professional networking and recruitment site.

Kate Batchelder is reading an advertorial article on a Condé Nast-owned website.

Sean Townsend is – well, we'll get to that.

Parras removes his lunch from his satchel, an energy drink plus tinfoil-wrapped cream-cheese bagel. He does a little chair yoga – rotates his underworked shoulder cuffs; leans side to side then to and fro, stretching his flank and lumbar areas.

Elsewhere on the network, he observes, Fred Honey is parasocially scrolling through Chloe Daley's Instagram grid from the remove of an anonymous burner account. He (Honey) does this every few hours, browses Daley's photos, videos and stories; has been tracking her wellness journey online now for months.

What must it be like, Parras wonders, to be pretty à la Chloe Daley? To receive low-hundreds of unique daily visitors to your social media profiles? To stare into a virtual mirror that tells you back how good you look? The images on her Instagram attest that it must be pretty nice.

Looking through her selfies, Parras ponders the quiddity of Daley's face. As with any kind of information, the more he's exposed to it, the less valuable it seems.

Remembering now that he has a professional obligation to the owner of the face displaying on his screen, Parras minimises the fantasy of images and rises from his chair. With a dead leg due to how long he's been sitting, he shambles upstairs like a zombie.

Since Nick Dwyer moved back with his parents in the spring, often mornings he'll carpool to work with Ray Bannon, whose weird, rigidly polite twins will sometimes – on the overnights for which Bannon's custody allows – be seated in the back of his mid-size hatchback. Bannon's children look like old men and barely ever say anything; just operate their handheld personal devices.

The air freshener in the car, which hangs from the rearview, is one of those mentholated, tree-shaped ones. Years of sunlight having long since dried the scent from it.

Fred Honey had a pleasant country upbringing which he feels he is now, in some way, paying for. In his youth, he was always quick to laughter; had a natural sympathy with musical instruments; matriculated into his high school's gifted and talented classes; played on sports teams, etc.

These days, in the post-onset of his thirties, he's becoming something of a loner: most weeknights he spends gaming solitarily or, occasionally, with his roommate; weekends he sees maybe an outside friend or two at an overcrowded/-priced bar for drinks.

To one of these friends, Honey recently remarked that he feels as though he's living his days stacked on top of one another.

When the friend asked Honey what, exactly, he meant, Honey said the main thing he's been feeling, lately, about his life is that he only really experiences each day beneath the overlay of all his previous ones, meaning his days are, in effect, thickening; weighted beneath the accreted, layered memory of every preceding, near-identical day.

Downplaying their nascent concern, the friend, who holds a BSc (Hons) in psychology, asked Honey if he could articulate the feeling in any further detail.

It's like the world is congealing around him, Honey said, sipping the foam head clean off his pint, 'due to, I think, constant repetition. As in, the more I do the same things over and over, the heavier the quality of the reality around me in which I do those things becomes. And then, the more things stay the same, the stucker I get inside that reality, the harder it gets for me to ever make any proper future changes. So, I'm grinding slowly to a halt, is what it feels like. Succumbing to entropy.' To settle the conversation with a joke, he added: 'In other words, I'm business-as-usual depressed.'

The friend laughed. They were thinking about how best to, non-invasively, get Honey to open up a little more, when he went ahead and opened up a little more entirely of his own accord.

'It's like – d'you ever feel like you used up all your good luck in life early on?'

The friend said no, not especially.

'Or, wait, at your work, d'you ever feel like something happened that morning, but then, when you go to think about it, you realise it actually happened, like, a week ago? Or a month – or even a year ago?'

The friend said sure.

'Well, see, that's exactly how I feel. Except I feel like it all the time.'

Only when the air conditioner in his executive office suddenly ceases noising overhead does Matt Maynard realise he's been hearing it non-stop for the past two hours. It's as though a new underlevel of silence has opened up beneath what he'd formerly thought of as silence's absolute baseline. As though now he can really think.

211

In the women's bathroom, Kate Batchelder applies a clot of face cream to the periorbital area beneath each eye and palpates it into her skin, which always feels devitalised by early afternoon.

Enter Chloe Daley and Leanne Kelly. The women all say hey; are standing in a row facing the bathroom's wall-width mirror, which hangs over three ovoid, surface-undermounted sinks.

Batchelder finds it vaguely humiliating to be framed in the same mirror as Daley and Kelly, next to whom she feels ugly, less-than. (In terms of the products they're marketed online, all three women fall within the same general age-range demographic.)

'How's it going, Kate?' Daley says, establishing first contact, being nice.

'Yeah, it's good, it's great,' Batchelder says, maybe too upbeat.

Daley applies a stylus of lip gloss to her lips and Kelly inhales from an e-cigarette, the tip of which glows the colour of embers. 'Did I tell you *he* called me the other night?' Kelly says, aiming her words at Daley and ignoring Batchelder.

Daley glances at Batchelder's reflection in the mirror, perhaps in apology, then head-turns to look at Kelly in real life. 'No, what'd he say?'

Daley and Kelly resume their semi-private conversation; Batchelder quietly moisturises her face. The division between them is clear.

Since high school, Batchelder has felt this dynamic reassert itself across numerous different contexts: beautiful women like Daley and beautiful-adjacent women like Kelly live in one reality, while she herself lives in another.

Screwing the lid back onto her tube of face cream, half-listening to Daley and Kelly's conversation, Batchelder thinks about the world's preference for its beautiful – its unjust prejudice against less attractive people. (How you know the prejudice is real is most people don't like to admit it exists.) People's lives are mostly drudgery, though, so it makes sense that, given the choice, they'd rather maximise their exposure to beautiful faces.

Funny: if someone were to portray Batchelder in a movie, they'd probably cast an actress more attractive than she is, but that way, you wouldn't get the full story of how it actually feels to be the protagonist in her life; her representation would necessarily beautify, and thereby undo, one of her main qualities – which is to say, her plainness.

Saying goodbye to Daley and nodding at Kelly, tube of face cream in hand, Batchelder exits the bathroom. It dawns on her, then, as she's walking back to her desk, that no, she was wrong – what she thought of before would never actually occur. Because if she were a character in a

213

movie, she realises, she wouldn't be the protagonist, but the friend.

They call it the canteen but it's just a room with three vending machines and a dozen circular foldaway dining tables set out atop an easy-wipe floor. The tables are all six-seaters with built-in stools undergirded to their bases via aluminium piping.

On one such table, Fred Honey, Sam Wendt, Perry Avery, Sean Townsend and Caroline Rochefort are seated together; a single corner stool remains empty.

Wendt says: 'Do any of you take vitamins?'

'I take a multivitamin,' Avery says. 'In the mornings.'

'I was taking these omega-3 softgels for a while,' Honey says, 'but now I don't take anything.'

'Shouldn't we all be taking vitamin D?' Rochefort says. 'Aren't we all supposed to be, like, chronically deficient in vitamin D?'

'I could give you some vitamin D,' Townsend says; winks at Rochefort, 'a *megadose* if you need.'

'Perfect,' Rochefort says, flatly.

'Wonderful, Sean,' Avery says, tearing an empty sugar sachet into halves, then into halves of halves.

'I did use to take a probiotic, though,' Townsend says, 'for my bowels.'

214

'How about maybe not while I'm eating,' Honey says, mouth filled with sandwich, although it's already too late; somehow, as he chews, he can taste the word 'bowels'.

Chloe Daley enters the room and the air therein seems to freshen. She waves at the five diners around the table; the diners all wave back. Honey goes from sitting at ease to sitting at attention.

Wendt says: 'I should start taking a multivitamin, I think.'

Townsend waits until Honey's taken another bite out of his right-angle BLT before saying: 'I heard zinc's supposed to increase the volume of your semen – is that what you're looking for?'

Honey tries to ignore Townsend; imagines himself far away.

'Really wonderful, Sean,' Avery says.

'What?' Townsend sips a strawful of orange juice from a not-for-individual-resale-sized carton.

In the back of the room, Chloe Daley operates the leftmost of the three vending machines, revealing a moment of skin around her waist as she bends down to collect whatever item the machine has just dispensed to her. Watching closely, Townsend says: 'Should I yell "Hubba-hubba" or "Boi-boi-oing"?'

'Has anyone spoken-to-slash-seen Henry Ontkean

today?' Honey says, staring determinedly into the remainder of his sandwich.

'I did, earlier,' Wendt says.

'His last day today,' Avery says, 'correct?'

'Correct,' Honey says. 'D'we have anything planned? Like, drinks?'

'No,' Rochefort says. 'We should make him dance before he leaves, though.'

'Dance?'

'D'you not remember the time he did the hustle at the Christmas party?'

Honey nods, not remembering, 'Oh right, yeah.'

'Fleet of foot, as I recall,' Avery says.

'Fat as fuck, as I recall,' Townsend says.

'Just wonderful, Sean.'

'Why do you talk like that?'

'Honey, honey, I was born this way. If it's such a problem, take it to human resources.'

Honey looks at Rochefort, who is human resources. 'How long till he's fired?'

Rochefort shrugs. 'When he stops being funny.'

'Seriously, though.'

'Okay then, *seriously*, he's fired.'

'You can't fire me,' Townsend deadpans, 'I quit.'

'Well, put him on a disciplinary or something. Surely there has to be a line.'

'What makes you think *you're* so special that *you* know where the line is?' Townsend says, evincing genuine irritation.

Honey holds his hands up surrender-style; side-eyes Daley as she exits the room. 'I'm just saying.'

'Oh, he's just saying, folks,' Townsend says, dragging on the straw of his juice carton, which runs audibly adry. 'He's just saying.'

Fred Honey has two major regrets, thoughts of which he alternates between for most of his days – the same way a restless sleeper alternates the side of their body they lie on at night.

Regret one: he shouldn't have broken up with X. That was a miserly, small-hearted thing to do; a rash decision whose gravity he didn't fully comprehend until after he'd made it – too late. Actually, he doesn't even think about X all that often around the office, because memories of her he likes to save up for the evenings, keep them special; but what X-related thing he *does* think about at work is their break-up itself: the Night of Tears, the back-and-forth of accusations, the eventual moving out.

Regret two: his chosen career path, or virtual absence thereof. After coasting through his critical theory degree with a 'just-tell-me-what-to-think' mentality and having attained, as a result, some disappointing, borderline grades, Honey spent the best part of the subsequent working decade pinballing between depressing temp positions at various interchangeable offices before taking on a permanent – and thus slightly more senior, slightly better paid, and slightly less depressing – role at PT&P. The thinking, there, was that, here, he might learn some useful, boring-but-transferable skills with which to branch-swing into a hopefully still better-paying and even less less-depressing eventual job. But it was two-plus years ago he started here, and look at him now: steady in middle management and never once promoted. Simultaneously too good for this place and somehow not good enough.

An interesting thing about leading a life you don't enjoy at all is: when every day is worse than the one preceding it – when you have no reason to hope for the future – the past gets comparatively better and better; seems actually to *improve*, despite its precondition of being set. Thanks to nostalgia's deepening quality, Honey has never felt more in love with X than he does now; his high school and university days have never seemed so magical.

The memories his brain autoplays from the happier stages of his life continue to upscale in definition and detail as the present becomes, increasingly, a barely processed blur. And even now, the Honey of the present, this far into his adulthood, still, like his younger self, only wishes some nice person would come along and tell him what to do.

What is it about being sedentary – about just sitting in the same place for an extended period of time – that makes you start to overthink things, drift into unhealthy rumination, develop strange obsessions? The cubicled body tends toward degeneracy, thinks Gigi Parras. Perhaps the human mind was evolved to move through space; requires the sensation of onrushing wind to know it is truly alive?

The hyperreal onscreen world is for-sure, no-contest preferable to the hostile grey reality in which the screens conveying that world actually, physically exist. Social media platforms have now fully supplanted the aspects of our lives they at first only seemed to depict.

Parras sits here watching the mass entrancement of his colleagues – day after day, hour after hour – hippocampi all engaged in computer uptime, consuming meaningless digital apparitions, intaking giant fluxes of information; gamblers transfixed by the slot machine's variable rewards.

Take yourself, for example: years ago, when you got your first smartphone, you checked it once every, what, like, couple of hours? Be honest – on many occasions, you forgot you even *owned* a smartphone; often, you had no idea where you'd left it.

Cut to now. When was the last time you read a full short story without, at some point, taking an intermission to check your device; refresh your feeds? Consider your forefathers/-mothers: did they feel it necessary to check their mailboxes every fifteen minutes? What, exactly, is going on here?

Just today, Parras himself got so bored reading an email on his laptop that he decided to take a few minutes' break away from his desk – only to realise, seconds later, he'd absently started reading the exact same email again on his smartphone.

Parras checks the date-and-time readout in the corner of his screen. Four hours of the workday remain. He tries not to think about Sean Townsend.

Fred Honey and Matt Maynard are each only a head taller than Chloe Daley, but standing outside in the smoking area with the both of them somehow has the weird combined effect of making her feel two heads shorter than either one of them.

'Y'know what?' Maynard says.

'Probably not,' Honey says, sulking; he'd thought it would be just him and Daley out here until Maynard tagged along.

'What?' says Daley.

'I don't think I've ever once spoken to Henry Ontkean.'

Daley puts her hand over her heart, 'I *love* Henry Ontkean. He's super shy, though.'

Honey leans against the elevated midsection of the smoking area's rarely used larchwood picnic bench. 'Isn't he a part of the insight team?'

'I think so.'

'Aren't you also a part of the insight team?'

'I'm in workflow,' Maynard says.

Honey nods and drifts into thinking about the company's different teams, then, after a while, forgets and tries to remember again whyever it was he started thinking about them in the first place – which hyperlinks him back around to the thought of Henry Ontkean.

Ontkean has worked at the office since way before Honey, and, in being such a constant, is indistinguishable in his mind from the décor of the office itself. (Difficult to imagine Ontkean as having any sort of extra-office life – which difficulty-in-imagining reminds Honey of how, as a child, he'd just assumed all his teachers lived at school.)

When Honey first started here, he and Ontkean shared a desk for a couple of weeks – had some nice enough times. He thinks through the fact that he hasn't yet seen Ontkean today; it's 1:45 p.m. already and he has a meeting 2–4. If Ontkean leaves early, they might miss each other completely.

'Borrow your lighter?' Daley says, her poorly hand-rolled cigarette having extinguished itself.

Honey underarm-throws Daley his miniature disposable; today's moderate-to-high winds make her hands something of a moving target. She ignites her cigarette with – then holds on to – the lighter; nice to think of her touching something Honey has also just touched.

Honey spends a moment imagining a depressingly far-fetched contrivance in which he and Daley fall in love: look into each other's eyes; 'Wanna get outta here?'

But she's talking to Maynard about something; Maynard having staged himself as closer to Daley than Honey, outshining him. Never should've leant against the bench, Honey chides himself. In matters of the heart, your blocking has to be inch-perfect.

Working here day after day, Honey thinks, is a lot like being forced to participate in a big dance you don't know the steps to – that you don't even *want* to know the steps to.

Already, Daley and Maynard are stubbing out the butts of their cigarettes. Daley turns to Honey and calls out: 'Catch.'

Honey makes a butterfingered attempt to grab the lighter as it arcs in mid-air; it bounces off his open palm and falls onto the smoking area's flame-retardant AstroTurf.

'Steady hands,' Daley says.

Dear Julia,

Well, I submitted that story to a few publications and got no takers, nor even any non-boilerplate rejection emails.

Rereading it, I think you were probably right about the ending. I guess it was kind of tacked-on and nonsensical, and didn't really serve the preceding narrative in any meaningful way.

I'm going to persevere with it, though, because I feel like I've got a good idea for a new

'Who's Julia?' Sean Townsend says, over Nick Dwyer's shoulder.

'What sorry?' Dwyer says without turning around, hurrying to minimise his web browser's open window, then to minimise several other open browser windows behind that one.

Sean Townsend looms. 'Who's Julia?'

'A friend.'

'*I submitted that story.*'

Dwyer forces a thin laugh. He's pretty sure Townsend is more than a decade older than him – why does he act like this?

'Let me read it.'

'What?'

'Your story,' Townsend says.

'Oh, no. I haven't even—'

'Don't hold out on me. Or else I'll tell everyone that some-thing you wrote got rejected from a load of—', he pauses to remember the word; clicks his fingers, '—*publications*.'

Dwyer swallows; raises his tongue into a roof-of-mouth position to begin forming the consonant half of the word 'no'.

'I'm just kidding,' Townsend says, 'this is all just a kid.'

Dwyer stares into his laptop, pretends to look busy and engaged. If Townsend's father wasn't such a big deal around here, he'd tell him to fuck off. 'I'm nearly finished with the presentation deck, Sean. I'll forward it to you and Perry in a bit.'

Townsend nods, 'Great,' his smile becoming a grimace. He wonders if he should even bother joking around any-more. People don't often get his sense of humour.

Over the course of the application process for this job, Nick Dwyer had to submit a CV and covering letter; sit a timed fourteen-question aptitude test online; answer a round of screening questions over the phone; attend two personal interviews and one group interview; provide a portfolio containing relevant samples of his work; sign a non-disclosure agreement; supply direct contact details for two former-employer referees.

The final question on the aptitude test was: 'What excites you the most about search engine optimisation?'

Kate Batchelder has developed superstitions around the way she operates the break-area coffee machine.

If she loads an Italian Smooth Roast filterpack into the appliance's filterpack insertion slot with her left hand, the resultant coffee will come out bitterer, she believes, than if she were to load it with her right – but she'll still drink it either way.

If the machine malfunctions mid-brew and she has to switch it off-then-on-again, it means she recently did something karmically wrong – for which transgression she'll force herself, as an act of penance, to call her mother after work.

Likewise, if the filterpack gets jammed in its loading slot; if the drip tray overflows; or if the machine's used filterpack bin gets clogged with empties, Batchelder attributes as the inconvenience's true cause some moral infraction of her own personal doing, and punishes herself accordingly.

On certain weeks, she calls her mother a lot.

Bathroom tile, ceiling tile, floor tile. Fred Honey is so super-bored, he's trying to think of every kind of tile there is.

Also in the meeting are Faye Taylor-Lewis, Chloe Daley and Sean Townsend.

Taylor-Lewis is presenting on teachable corporate strategies for creating workplace cultures that motivate their employees to do better; she's been presenting now, uninterrupted, for twenty-eight minutes.

Westering late-afternoon sunlight filters in slices through the blinds of the room's lone window.

Patio tile. Looks at the clock. Twenty-nine minutes, uninterrupted.

Taylor-Lewis's voice is clarinet-like; rich and low. Surely, Townsend thinks, all this could've been communicated more effectively via email; surely she's aware that none of this is of actual value, just busywork.

Townsend feels the makings of a tension headache; presses his fingertips medium-hard into his closed eyes – the nearest you can safely get to touching your own brain.

Daley not-so-surreptitiously operates her smartphone beneath the meeting-room table. Honey watches her; Taylor-Lewis watches him watching her, while she (Taylor-Lewis) continues to orate.

As Daley leans forward and replaces her smartphone face-down atop the table, Honey notices that the screen of his own smartphone – face-up, in front of him, across the same table – appears, briefly, to have illuminated; likely with a new message notification, possibly one from Daley.

This possibility makes the next few moments of Honey's life feel worth living; he reaches over and collects his smartphone, then, once he's actuated its side button, realises he's received no such notification at all – that the light source he observed playing across the device's screen was, in fact, external to the device itself; a figment of changing shadow, probably the result of Daley's movements. Honey slides down in his chair a little; recommences the same mood he was in before.

Thirty minutes. Roof tile.

Perry Avery knocks on the door.

'Yo,' comes the answer from inside.

As Avery enters Matt Maynard's office, a converging of airflows between rooms raises the corners of the loose papers on Maynard's desk like a haunting. 'Hey Matt,' Avery says.

Maynard has his feet up on his desk, against which his torso also leans, sideways on. He wears a wireless, white earphone in one ear, and stares at his laptop's screen for the entirety of this interaction.

'Nick's finalised the copy amends in the presentation deck,' Avery says. 'I've just sped-read through; looks good. I'll forward it to you and Ban-man any minute.'

'Great work as per, Per,' Maynard says.

Avery has long imagined something insectoid, mantis-like, lives beneath Maynard's skin. 'No worries, Matt.'

'Suck my fucking dick while you're at it,' Maynard says, after Avery has departed from the room and closed the door behind him.

Dream in which Caroline Rochefort has reverse-cowgirl-position sex with her adult son.

Dream in which Chris Newland pulls out his teeth, one by one, from the incisors back.

Dream in which Ray Bannon inherits a fortune.

Dream in which Nick Dwyer has to retake his final year of high school at age twenty-eight due to an administrative error.

Dream in which Leanne Kelly is sentenced to life in prison without trial or the possibility of parole.

Dream in which Gigi Parras is strangled to near-death by Sean Townsend onstage in a live event setting.

Light bleeds pinkly through Sean Townsend's closed eyelids; his headache is really going at it now.

Chloe Daley and Faye Taylor-Lewis are talking about past internal communications campaigns. Fred Honey has interjected maybe three or four times with related insights of his own, none of which have proven particularly insightful.

In her capacity as the meeting's facilitator, Taylor-Lewis involves Townsend in the group discussion. 'Sean, d'you have any skillshares based on the points we've covered so far?'

Backfooted at being summoned to speak after having not listened to a single word Taylor-Lewis said during her whole presentation, Townsend recovers quickly from inattention to attention. 'Well, I think,' he says, spacing his words evenly apart as if they've been deeply considered, 'there's already so much to unpack.'

Perfectly timed: a knock on the door; Caroline Rochefort steps sideways into the room. 'Hi, how long are you guys booked in here for?'

Taylor-Lewis checks her thin silver wristwatch: 'Another hour, I'm afraid.'

Expression of forbearance on Rochefort's face; 'Okay, no worries'; she sidesteps back out of the room.

Honey stares at the door after Rochefort closes it.

Daley uncrosses and recrosses her legs the opposite way.

Grateful for the interruption, Townsend places the index and middle fingers of his right hand on his right temple; acts like he's wrapping up where he left off. 'Anyhow, Faye, you've done some stellar work here. It seriously sounds fantastic.'

Taylor-Lewis clicks her retractable rollerball pen; leans in toward Townsend. 'But what about it *specifically* sounds fantastic?'

'And then, tell Nick what happened next,' Ray Bannon says, directing Leanne Kelly to retell the anecdote to Nick Dwyer properly, the way he's already heard it.

Thus far, Kelly and her friends have gone to a club where one of the friends has given her number to a good-looking guy.

Thinking the story was going to be about an awful night out, Dwyer has already fake-laughed multiple times at Kelly's descriptions of the club, although now it appears the story is winding around to being about something else entirely, and that Kelly didn't even think the club was bad.

'So,' Kelly continues, 'we end up getting pretty boozed, yadda-yadda-ya, the night trails off and everyone goes home. Then, after that, my friend keeps texting this *guy*.'

This seems like a natural resting point in the story to interject with something, so Dwyer goes: 'Uh-oh,' and Bannon laughs without opening his mouth.

They are, the three of them, loitering in the corridor that connects the ground floor's main office space to the canteen.

Dwyer is glad to have gotten involved in this conversation while holding a cup of coffee – it gives him a nice displacement activity to continually reorient his thoughts toward; something to keep busy his hands, like how, in his drinking days, he used to hold a beer.

It transpires that Kelly's friend has been texting – and ultimately arranged a date with – the good-looking guy whom she met at the club, two weeks ago now in the story's timeline. 'And so, she goes to this bar, and she waits for, like, however long, and then this really, like, gross-looking guy comes and approaches her.'

Bannon and Kelly share a knowing look; it is clear this escalating story beat will prove pivotal to the anecdote's overall dramatic structure.

'Okay,' Dwyer says at half-speed, like he's putting all the pieces together.

'And the *guy*,' Bannon says, as a prompt.

'He looks awful. He's dressed like shit, and all his features are, like, crowded together in the middle of his face.'

'Uh-huh.' Dwyer throws back the last, gone-cold centimetre of his Italian Smooth Roast – disgusting.

'And so, he goes over to my friend, this guy, and says, y'know, hi, I'm here to meet up with you, he knows her name and everything, and orders them both a drink. And my friend's thinking, uh, y'know, like, alarm bells, something's definitely up here, how did I ever think this guy was good-looking?'

'And *so*,' Bannon says.

231

Dwyer feels sort of bad for Kelly here, he knows well the pressure of having to imitate the spontaneity of an anecdote's former telling; how careful one must be not to add/subtract any superfluous/vital details that might compromise the story's final impact.

'And so, my friend and this guy are sitting down, and they do the whole, like, nice-to-re-meet-you thing, but in her head, she's thinking the whole time about, like, how much energy she's wasted texting this creepy-looking guy for the last couple of weeks. And so, eventually, she brings it up, and says, uh, I'm really sorry, but like, you don't look at all how I remember you from the night at the club. And the guy says—'

Bannon looks sidelong at Dwyer; checks he's paying adequate attention.

'—He says, what d'you mean, at the club? She goes, at the club where I gave you my number, and he goes, I didn't meet you at any club. We met after you puked on the pavement while you were waiting for the nightbus. I just helped you up off the floor and you told me I was a hero and insisted I take your number. Remember? He's like: what, were you expecting someone else?'

Cue long moment of Dwyer waiting for some kind of punchline, then realising that the punchline has already been and gone. 'Wow,' he says, 'that's crazy.'

Bannon is practically falling over himself laughing.

'So, wait, there were two different people? Two guys?'

'Yeah,' Kelly says, a little self-conscious, 'I don't know, maybe you had to be there. I mean, there when I told Ray the first time.'

'No, no,' Dwyer says, 'it's definitely crazy.'

They laugh; are all briefly in solidarity laughing. It feels good to have a good feeling and share it – even if, Dwyer thinks, Kelly's story did have obvious third-act pacing flaws.

A kind of Stockholm syndrome has set in where Fred Honey can no longer imagine a life beyond this meeting room and feels as though he'll only ever know the people who are here with him inside of it.

He could marry and grow old with Chloe Daley, no problem, and believes Faye Taylor-Lewis and Sean Townsend could probably find a way to chum around together, if they only tried. The four of them might reconstruct some kind of from-scratch primitive society: hunt, gather, forage and barter.

In her presentation, Taylor-Lewis uses the word 'penalise', which resurfaces Honey back into the present and leads him to make fugitive eye contact with Townsend, from whom he then looks promptly away, retreating again into an imagined realm of high fantasy.

Townsend, meanwhile, is glad he obviously isn't the only one who helplessly thinks the word 'penis' when he hears the word 'penalise'. He wonders now if the women are also thinking about penises.

He tries, but he can't even imagine what Taylor-Lewis's interior monologue must be like – she's one of those people who's so normal she kind of seems insane. And anyway, it's far more entertaining to imagine whatever Daley's thinking about.

She always looks relatably bored, Daley does, but there's no way she can have accessed the same kinds of full-on lonely-guy boredom as Townsend has in his life. She's never attended, say, a working men's club in the mid-afternoon, nor a strip club on a midweek night. The world spares the beautiful from its most soul-crushing experiences.

Or maybe that's wrong, Townsend thinks; performing such a bland, functionary role as Daley's around this office must surely have its own way of corroding the spirit.

Speaking of which, Townsend has intentionally not-checked the time for at least – going by his body clock – half an hour. He's been holding off to have something to look forward to; waiting for what feels like a nice round number of minutes to pass before he takes another incremental measure of the meeting's slow progress.

Earlier, when Caroline Rochefort intruded into the

room and Taylor-Lewis said they still had an hour left booked in, Townsend checked his watch in disbelief; he is confident – *certain*, even – that over half an hour has elapsed since then.

He checks his watch again and is crushed to learn that in reality only twelve minutes have gone by, meaning there remain, however implausibly, a further forty-eight minutes of meeting to endure.

Determined to reclaim at least some of this dead time, Townsend double-taps his laptop's trackpad, tilts its display toward him a few degrees, and, in the moment before the device's operating system awakens, catches sight of his own, sad reflection in the standby-mode monitor's panel of lifeless dark.

After his login screen has booted and he's entered his password, Townsend ensures his laptop is muted; performs a casual blind-spot check over each shoulder – reassured, now, that the screen's contents are visible only to himself.

Bypassing his every reasonable precaution not to do this (and with this boundary transgression functioning as its own reward), nodding along all the while as Taylor-Lewis continues speaking, Townsend cedes control to an overriding impulse and opens an incognito window in his web browser.

Who are you when nobody's watching? Or at least, when you think nobody's watching – when you're fairly sure there's no one standing over your shoulder, within viewing range of your screen?

You assume, of course, that you'd be able to tell if somebody was watching over you; that, if there were one, you'd immediately sense the presence of an intruder in the room.

Although Sean Townsend occupies a physically unoverseeable desk in one of the office's corner workstations, he has, unknowingly, been subject to close surveillance now for weeks, going on months. Which is why he's at risk of being fired without severance for watching pornography via his company laptop on company time.

This week alone, Gigi Parras has clocked Townsend's overall in-office pornography consumption at just shy of six hours in aggregate – almost eighty median minutes'-worth of jiggling, clapping and gyrating body parts each working day.

Some of-interest titles Parras has noted Townsend watching recently: '45-Minute Try Not To Cum Challenge'; 'Stepdaughter Sucks Off Stepdad and His Five Fat Horny Friends'; 'My Stepmother Got Stuck Under the Table and I Banged Her'; 'Dare Dorm'; 'Ebony Dare Dorm'; 'The Loneliness of the Big-Titted Military Wife'; 'Inside the Czech Sauna'; 'Memoirs of a Human Succubus'.

To say nothing of the fact that most of the videos appear to have been hosted illegally and accessed in contravention of their original copyright holders' terms of licence, Townsend's viewership of the videos easily classifies as a violation of PT&P's Degrading Environment Policy, which constitutes a Fireable Misdemeanour – meaning, if he so wished, Parras could have him dismissed.

Couple of problems there, though:

1. How could Parras realistically prove Townsend has viewed the videos without at least partway implicating himself and his personal surveillance project?

2. Does the office even have a linear, formal process for the registration of grievances? Parras can't remember a single time he's seen it done before. (In a different workplace, he might file a complaint with HR, but here, he knows, he'd just get an eyeroll or a laugh or maybe both from Caroline Rochefort, plus probably a follow-up intimidation email from Townsend's father, because . . .)

3. There's also a third issue, which is that Old Man Townsend, one of PT&P's original co-founders, still occupies a substantial – if, given a recent illness, increasingly spectral – presence on the company's board of directors.

(And, let's altogether avoid getting into a hypothetical issue '4.' which would be: Does Parras even really want to see Townsend – a guy he can, admittedly, barely stand – lose his job?)

Still, a colleague jacking it at work is clearly something you can't just ignore. The good-person thing to do would obviously be to do something – which, in this specific circumstance, is what, exactly?

After weeks of deliberation, Parras has decided to take matters into his own hands; deal with the situation head-on. If he won't enforce company standards, after all, who will?

His new plan is to stake out Townsend's user profile for the rest of the day, and on into next week if he has to. Then, when Townsend inevitably watches some afternoon hardcore, he'll inform him that the office's security system has detected either malware or spyware on his laptop – make up some reasonable, anti-virus-y-sounding lie; give him a stern-but-tactful talking-to about his browsing habits. Stage a mini-intervention, almost. Not a whole big thing, no unnecessary drama. Just a conversation, like between adults.

Straining the already-pretty-unclear definition of what constitutes 'work' in the modern workplace, Sam Wendt is braindeadly completing the self-assessment section of his biannual performance review form.

Total make-work; a legit charade; a task of zero real-world import – Wendt usually tries not to be too cynical about this kind of thing but, like, c'mon.

What has my life come to if forms like this are all I have to occupy my time with? Wendt thinks. Further thoughts of a similarly depressive index soon start welling up behind that initial thought, which Wendt successfully blocks out by marshalling the line of his thinking back toward the task at hand.

What three targets can you set for yourself to ensure you progress within your role over the next six months? the performance review form says. Wendt's lips move as he reads the question, then rereads the question several times over to delay actually having to answer it.

He slips off his loafers under his desk and gives his socked feet some air; yawns and full-length-extends his arms out in front of him.

Come to think of it, right now, things really aren't so bad. It's late afternoon and the day is already on its down-hill trajectory – the weekend is coming into view. Outside, it looks to be nice enough weather. Listen. The crows are barking in their trees.

Spin-the-bottle game, Tina Clarke's house, a Friday night in 2001. Kate Batchelder is twelve years old.

Kate Batchelder has only been invited to play because Mikey Wardell's mother childminds her on the evenings when Kate's own mother pulls a late or double shift. (The inverse of this situation also happens sometimes, where Mikey Wardell is collected from school and childminded by Kate's mother while Mikey's mother has work.) Through the transitive property of their mothers' dealings, Mikey's invitation to Tina Clarke's house tonight has also been extended to Kate – Mikey's mother will pick them both up at 7:30.

Important to know: the young Batchelder has been in love with the young Wardell now for years. She loves his long eyelashes; his slight, boy's shoulders; she even loves when he does that double-jointed, hitchhiker's-thumb thing, which she finds gross in the abstract but special on him. Her happiest life moments have all been playing Beanie Babies and watching Friday-evening TV together with her mother and Mikey – although, lately, they've been more distant with each other, which Kate interprets as a symptom of their mutual, pubescent shyness.

At school, Kate almost never interacts with Mikey, nor with the likes of Tina Clarke – she spends most of her lunches and breaktimes in the library with Ms Withers. Fine by Kate: she loves to read, and the school's library has the entire series of *Sweet Valley High* books, whose simulations of the melodramas of adolescent life are more than enough for her, socially. Also, Ms Withers has a lovely smile and a gentle way; Kate can always confide in her.

Excited as she is to attend a gathering at Tina's, so too does Kate feel like a hanger-on. If I make eye contact with as few people as possible, she thinks, it'll be like I'm not even here.

She's sitting in the spin-the-bottle circle on the carpet next to Mikey, who hasn't looked at her a single time all evening. (The carpet in Tina's parents' semi-furnished basement has those little wiry hairs matted into it, just like the carpet at school does – polypropylene loop pile – which is also the same type of carpet that'll, next year, be unrolled over the floors of PT&P's newly established offices.) A couple of the other boys, Kate can't help but notice, have been making fun of her, but she's quick to recall something consolatory Ms Withers once told her: that often, bullies are the kids with the saddest home lives.

Anyway, she still feels excited to take part in the game – even if it's just as a bystander, which, honestly, she prefers. The grown-ups of the house are upstairs, and there's a freewheeling air of hormonal possibility in the room. Disc two of *Now That's What I Call Music! 49* plays in the background. In spite of herself, Kate is doing her happiest smile.

Of the girls, Tina's spun the bottle the most times, and has kissed Max Boddely, Saf Spencer and Will Sims – exempting Mikey, that's every boy in attendance. Charlie Patrick has kissed Saf Spencer twice. Allison Faiers has kissed Max Boddely and Mikey – which latter kiss almost broke Kate's heart, but she knew to take in good humour.

Kate declines to spin every time it's her turn – she's seen how all the boys look at her and, honestly, she knows if she did spin, the bottle would land right on Will Sims, easily the basement's least-promising-looking suitor, but also, for that reason, probably the one she most deserves. She does not want her first kiss to be with him.

Now the girls have had their goes and the boys are spinning. Max Boddely takes first turn and it lands on Mikey – everyone laughs and calls Max a homo. He respins, and the bottle lands on Allison Faiers. They kiss using tongues. All the kids are repulsed and compelled in equal measure; they cheer and scream – Tina has to yell at them shut up, shut up, shut up.

Saf Spencer spins; the bottle lands on Kate. He beams at her – genuine, merciful – then, without saying anything, respins. He lands on Charlie Patrick, and administers to her a nervous, taught-lipped peck.

Mikey goes next. Kate isn't so bold as to actively wish for his bottle-spin to select her, she only hopes that it doesn't land on Tina, who she's pretty sure has a thing for Mikey and could easily steal him away.

The bottle is spinning now – Kate's whole happiness depends upon a roulette of pure, unweighted chance; if there is a God, she prays He will intervene.

And, unbelievably, He does intervene.

Before it even happens, Kate understands it's happening – yes, the bottle; it's slowing down; one last revolution of the circle, which now it's fulfilled, and, yes, yes, it's pointing directly at her.

'Oh my god'; 'Wait till the rest of class hears about this'; 'Kiss, kiss, kiss.'

Mikey looks at everyone in the basement who isn't Kate. Seconds pass; a lengthy indecision. Kate makes sure to relax, be casual, so as not to alarm Mikey with any over-obvious indication of the rawness of her love for him. He still hasn't leant sideways to initiate a kiss, but neither has he yet leant forwardways to retake his turn.

Max, Saf, Will, Charlie and Allison keep chanting, 'Kiss'; Tina tells them all to shut up.

Kate channels the confidence of *Sweet Valley High*'s protagonist Jessica Wakefield (but is careful not to get overconfident, which is so often Jessica's undoing), and leans in toward Mikey with her face slightly upturned.

'Close your eyes,' Mikey instructs her, still looking elsewhere, and she does.

Eyes tightly shut; everything fully black.

Will's voice goes, 'Holy shit.'

First, the awareness of spit hitting her face; next, the registration of the awareness of spit hitting her face; then, at an adrenaline-induced delay, the sound of Mikey spitting in her face. Finally, a chorus of adolescent group laughter.

Before she even thinks to open her eyes, Kate assembles an expression like she's in on the joke – like: good one, Mikey – as though she were only inhabiting the severest humiliation of her poor little life ironically. Like: who, *moi?* Like: you think you dashed *my* hopes? *Très* funny, Mikey. Nice try.

Her eyes still closed, the insults start surround-sounding her – the voices in the room all blurring together as one: 'Drink spit!'; 'Bullseye!'; 'Dumb bitch!'; 'What a cow!' Multiple fresh spits land on her face from different directions.

Fully isolable at the centre of the ring of voices, though, comes Mikey's, amused: 'As if I'd kiss you. You're way too ugly.'

Kate keeps her eyes closed and absorbs it all; feigning unawareness and not-taking-any-notice, which possibly only makes the other kids angrier and meaner. Her strategy is just to keep on happy-smiling; to simply, and with grace, endure the moment, which feels like it goes on for several minutes, and, perhaps, in reality, it does.

It's okay; it's natural; to be honest she deserves it: they've caught her in the act of getting too merry, and now they must drag her back down to reality; reassert her symbolic place. People are repulsed by the weak and the ugly, and Kate remembers now she is both of those things. She'll be cautious to never forget either again.

When she reopens her eyes, after all the others have dispersed to consort in smaller groups, she's so dazed, she won't even think to cry until after Mikey's mother has dropped her home; until after she's told her own mother she had a nice time; until much later, when her mother kneels down by her bedside to sing the tuck-in-goodnight song – only, instead of starting to sing like normal, asks her in a high voice: 'Katie, sweetie, did something happen with your friends?'

While certainly not the worst thing that's ever happened to Kate, somehow, almost two decades later, it is still probably the most demoralising thing. So much in her life she's forgiven and forgotten – her mother's moods, her father's remarriages – but, despite its long-pastness, this memory still holds sway over her; it remains one of the most familiar, cyclically recurrent landmarks in the terrain of her thinking, probably because it was the moment at which she learned so many of life's cruellest lessons at once.

Obviously, she holds none of the persons involved in any contempt; she bears no grudges, they were all but children then. Weirdly, Allison Faiers works as a carer now, and is on the team of staff that looks after Kate's mother.

On a recent weekend visit, Kate ran into Allison in the long-term mental health facility's reception area. 'Your mother talks about you so much,' Allison said – her face has gotten larger, but still contains intact all its pretty, younger features; the effect is of her childhood face being faintly watermarked by a generic, adult one.

'You as well,' Kate said, 'she thinks you're wonderful.'

'So, how's it going?' Allison said. 'How have—' she started, searched around, then laughed, '—well, how've the years been?'

And to this, what could Kate even say.

In the break area, Sean Townsend is sitting alone, waggling a spoon pinched between his thumb and forefinger in such a way as to make it appear bendy.

'Can I borrow you for five minutes?' No longer alone; Gigi Parras is craning his neck around the area's doorless doorway. 'In my office?'

'I'm kind of in the middle of perfecting an artform.'

'Something we need to talk about.'

'Save us the effort and let's talk here.'

Parras's shoulders, then arms, torso, legs and feet follow his head into the area. 'Sort of private.'

'Well, shall we book in a one-to-one next week?'

'Now's better.'

'Is it a hundred per cent necessary? I've got a post-Faye-T.-L.-meeting headache.'

'I'll be quick.'

'And you're *sure* it can't wait?'

A little severely: 'It's gone half four and I've got to sign off Ontkean's laptop before close, so no.'

Townsend sighs into a yawn; still doing the spoon thing: 'What happened with the girl who was supposed to be replacing Ontkean? The redhead?'

'Redhead' is among Townsend's most frequently used search terms on adult websites; Parras cringes now to hear him say it.

'I heard she had mental problems.'

'Sounds about right.' Townsend purrs out a muffled fart into the chair. He rises; sets about reconfiguring his idea of what the final hour of his working week will look like. 'Alright,' he says, 'put me in the firing line.'

At no other hour of the day does the atmosphere of the modern office feel so classroom-like as in its final one. The fact you can't just up and leave, even when you have nothing to do, is insane.

Chris Newland could really do with getting home early

247

this evening, and considers saying so to his deskmate, Perry Avery. He doesn't, though – Avery still looks to be working at least halfway-hard.

Viewed some ways, you could convincingly make the case that Newland has formatted his entire personality around being able to tolerate the feeling of just sitting here, letting his precious life-moments pass him by like it doesn't mean anything. But it *does* mean something, he thinks now, realising he's been holding his breath for the last few moments. It has to.

Under the pretence of helping himself to another of Henry Ontkean's leaving pastries from the break area, Fred Honey walks over to check up on Chloe Daley, whose desk is located en route. He rounds a corner and sees she's laughingly engaged in conversation with Matt Maynard.

Honey is halfway turned around again and walking away when he hears Maynard saying, deliberately loudly: 'Anyway, you want to watch out for that old Fred Honey, he's a nasty piece of work.'

Honey turns back around; depleting his final reserves of self-respect as he joins in with the routine: 'Hey, I heard that.'

'Sorry, Fred,' Maynard says. 'Caught us talking about you.'

'So, what's the verdict?' Fred says.

'Re: you?'

'You do *not* want to know,' Daley says, all this joking bordering on vaudevillian.

'Don't shrug; out with it.'

'We think you're no good,' Maynard says, shrugging for a second time.

'A scoundrel,' Daley insists.

'That sounds like me to me. So, what's going on?'

'Nothing,' Daley says.

'Just a casual Friday afternoon tête-à-t—'

'Any news?'

'No news.'

'Either of you seen Henry Ontkean anywhere?'

'Earlier,' Maynard says. 'But not for a while.'

Daley rolls, on the casters of her desk chair, back over to her desk; consults the officewide shared calendar on her laptop's email software. 'He's due to decommission his laptop with Gigi at five, meaning he'll be around still.'

'Cool cool cool.'

'Got a big, emotional farewell planned?' Maynard says.

Why is Maynard even here, Honey thinks. He is a side-character taking up valuable space in the main narrative of events. 'I guess.'

'Can't spend your whole life guessing, Fred.' At every opportunity, Maynard validates all the bad feelings Honey has about him. Notice how, even when he's properly smiling, his face exhibits only minimal change.

Honey considers beclowning Maynard back someway, but his degree of personal investment in this conversation has critically waned – besides, the rules of engagement when it comes to a subordinate making fun of a superior constitute a grey area in office politics. Now he actually kind of does want a pastry.

'Well, you two stay out of trouble,' Honey says, careful not to outlet his private disappointment over this whole failed interaction.

'Oh, we will,' Maynard says; friendly in a way that's hard to believe.

As Honey reaches the break area, the arpeggiating singsong of Daley's laugh can be heard from as many as ten desks away.

From his career in sales, Sean Townsend has learned whichever individual addresses the other first in a two-person meeting adopts the subordinate role for the remainder of that interaction. Which is why, here in Gigi Parras's office, he's stayed silent since sitting down.

He feigns not knowing what this is even about, although he's pretty sure he does know what this is about. Fingers interlaced in lap, casual; looking all around the low-ceilinged, tiny-windowed basement without taking much in; Parras, seated opposite, just clack-clacking away at his laptop.

Nothing out of place here save for a half-eaten cream-cheese bagel on Parras's desk. When Townsend imagines Parras's home life, he imagines it as frigid and boring, bleak and museumy: commemorative plates; collectible figurines; cabinets of items you can't touch.

Parras's continuous leg-jogging under his desk sounds like two dogs fucking without barking – Townsend having recently seen footage of this exact phenomenon. Even the way he sits at his desk is annoying; his ramrod-straight, upright-piano-player posture.

For Parras, the issue now is he can't think of what to say – hence why he's sitting here pretending to operate his computer, waiting until something occurs to him.

He mostly just feels sorry for Townsend, whose desires have been configured and inflated by commercial logics – subject to predatory algorithms that show you what you want before you even know you want it yourself. He can empathise with Townsend's seeking out some insulation from the cold surface of reality, his wanting to ease the tension of time's passing.

Still, where to start with a thing like this? What conversational gateway will get them into the discussion they need to have? Maybe he should just say nothing – let Townsend speak for himself.

He swivels toward Townsend on his executive leather-backed desk chair; steeples his forefingers together and rests them against his lips. He pauses, then allows the pause to extend. Townsend stirs in his seat a little; props his elbows up on its armrests. Each one thinking he could sit here forever, until the other speaks first.

Kate Batchelder is leaving the office. She secures her laptop in its weekend storage locker, clads herself in her coat and hat, sings 'Buh-bye' to no one in particular, and exits.

Matt Maynard, watching her leave, reflects that women who wear hats often seem, in his opinion, ill-adjusted to reality.

The custodians commence their weekly final clean-up of the building. Otherwise, no signs of life in the first-floor meeting room; the ground-floor meeting room; the foyer; the canteen.

Every time you close your eyes another day goes by.

See your co-workers single-filing out of the office, released to their nearby homes. Another Friday evening of status quo.

Fred Honey looks out of a second-storey window at the nothing-much-to-see; the sun an hour from setting over the business park.

He returns to Henry Ontkean's desk, which remains uncleared. It is so like Ontkean to wait until after work hours to empty his desk on his last day.

Honey motions to withdraw his smartphone from his trouser pocket, only to be reminded – by his hand landing flat against his outer thigh – that he left the device on his own desk, located one floor below. Waiting for Ontkean with nothing around to distract him makes Honey feel passive, bridal.

There is a certain pathos to the novelty items that adorn Ontkean's desk: the stuffed-animal pencil case; the multi-coloured stationery organiser; the lei of artificial flowers. Something about the objects – their mass-produced, upward attempts toward generating consumer delight – makes Honey feel quite sad, overcome. In this moment, he shuts his eyes. The next, they're open again.

Now they're scanning Ontkean's leaving card, which stands upright by his in-tray, extracted from its envelope. *Keep in touch – F.H.*

He is reading the card's other, more outwardly affectionate entries when Ontkean lumbers into, then across, the room.

'Fred, hi?'

253

Honey looks up from the card and rises quickly from where he's been sitting on the edge of Ontkean's desk. Former desk. 'Henry. I didn't see you yet today.'

'Oh man,' Ontkean says, semi-out-of-breath, leaning an arm's-worth of his heft against the back of his former desk chair, 'it ended up being one of *those*. My exit interview went on and on, then Gigi was supposed to decommission my laptop but, by the sounds of things, he had something weird going on in his office, so I just left it outside his door. *Then* I had to upskill a bunch of people on some process stuff no one other than me even understands.' He runs a heavy hand through his schoolboy's flop of blonde hair – not exactly blonde but colourless, clear-looking.

'Well, that's why you're so valuable,' Honey says, enjoying Ontkean's clement, panda-like presence.

'They never seem to realise how valuable you are *while* you're working here, though.'

'True.' Already remembering the answer to this question before he's finished asking it: 'Where is it you're headed again?' He adds, 'Breavemann, right?'

'Actually, no. I'm just going to live in the middle of the woods.'

'Oh. D'you know anyone out there who's hiring?'

Ontkean laughs. 'Yeah, Breavemann. That's correct.'

'Major leagues,' Honey says.

'Certainly a step up,' Ontkean says, then catches himself. 'Not that—'

'No no, I know.'

'—because PT&P is a great—'

'It's—'

'—a great place to work.'

Honey shrugs. 'I was just thinking earlier. My ex-girlfriend always used to say this place makes me miserable.'

A look crosses Honey's face. The most personal conversation he and Ontkean have had before was once when they talked about movies.

'And does it?'

'Yeah.'

'How miserable?'

Honey bobs his head from side to side. 'Reasonably.'

'Well, you could certainly do a lot worse,' Ontkean says.

'Believe me, I have done a lot worse. Will you miss it?'

'I'll miss the people.'

'Everyone says that.'

'Doesn't make it untrue.'

'Yeah, and then they say that, also.'

'Obviously if I hear of any positions going at Breavemann—'

'That's kind.'

The conversation reaches a logical point of terminus.

'But anyway, congratulations.'

'Thanks,' Ontkean says, 'for stopping by.'

'Yep.'

'Well.'

The men shake hands – Ontkean's is mascot-sized – then they each take a single step back from the handshake. The moment is oddly sensitising; Honey tries to think of a reference for how to act in this situation.

'You'll turn it around, Fred,' Ontkean says, smiling.

Honey slips his hands into his pockets. He will miss the way – when Ontkean smiles at a joke or at even simply being talked to – the smile lasts on his face for a long time after, like a hole that's been pushed into dough. 'Take care, Henry,' he says.

Walking downstairs, the blood in Honey's head either surges or else just seems to surge; his face goes both sparkling and numb. He feels this tight, pre-cry pressure behind his eyes, leans for a moment against the banister and waits for it to subside.

The weekend has begun. As he emerges from the stairwell into the first floor's main work area, he thinks about all the weekends destined to follow on from this one, then about the many long workweeks that will precede those. Every hour of his life he feeds unchangingly into a cosmic timesheet, and that time is billable back only to himself.

Standing by his desk, he remembers from cognitive behavioural therapy a trick for out-thinking the mechanism of his negative thinking – he observes and labels his catastrophising for what it is: just noise, just words.

Imagine comfort, he tells himself.

Imagine acceptance.

Now imagine not having a single regret.

Now imagine a modest homestead filled with people you love.

Now imagine stepping outside into a summery and tranquil meadow – visualise your face rinsed in daylight.

Now imagine commuting to your job on a Monday morning via private or public transport; you are running neither early nor late, everything is perfectly on time; there are many interesting and loving new messages for you to read on your smartphone if you so wish, and you do; the weather is exactly how you want it to be; you are wearing clothes that make you feel like the best version of yourself; you are holding, perhaps, a cup of your favourite morning beverage – arriving into the office, your co-workers are all so glad to see you; they smile at you, warmly, in greeting. Welcome back.

The Foreseeable

'Okay, this one's for real,' Julia said, the artifacting visual of her face lagging momentarily behind the clipping audio of her voice; for the duration of our FaceTime, sound and image would come unsynced whenever she moved her smartphone. 'I can feel it.'

'Alright,' I said, raising my voice, as though it might transmit any clearer over so weak a signal that way, 'but if it disconnects again, I'll just normal-call you. Otherwise we'll keep getting our wires crossed.'

Julia's network coverage dropped out frequently at her mother's house – often when she was mid-sentence, seemingly for dramatic effect. This was our third attempt at FaceTiming tonight, and our third overall night of Face-Timing in just under as many months. Aside from when we'd encountered one another in the city the previous spring – and exempting the steady email and text correspondence we'd maintained since then – Julia and I had been estranged now for almost four years.

It was a Friday – not that, in the new temporality, the names of days still signified their original meanings. 'So, what's going on,' I said. 'Big weekend plans?'

Julia laughed, and I got to experience her laughter. 'Rumour has it there'll be a supermarket pilgrimage tomorrow.'

'I'm jealous,' I said, 'I've already shopped my one shop this week.'

'Y'know, you can still grocery-shop whenever you want. It isn't, like, prohibited.'

'Not the way my mother sees it.'

'Aha. And whatever your mother says goes.'

I cleared my throat, then cleared it again, then coughed. 'Exactly.'

Julia and I had started FaceTiming back when the epidemic first inflection-pointed into a pandemic. In our calls, we mostly discussed topics that were low-to-the-ground and banal: conveniences we missed; films we'd seen; the extended universe of our mutual friends. Rarely did we talk about the virus directly – or about the unprecedented peacetime measures being undertaken to contain its spread – although, of course, it dominated our conversations, not as their subject, but as their subtext and foundation; as the very reason for our calling.

Julia asked what I'd been doing today and I said writing, same as always. I put the question back to her and she answered, glumly: 'Just making the most of my enforced leisure time.' She asked if it was raining where I was and I checked my window and reported no.

It was the magic hour of an early-summer evening; I was in my desk chair with my feet on my desk. The window beside me overlooked the field of air one storey above my parents' garden. The setting sun beyond that window cast my bedroom in strawberry-blonde light; onscreen, I noticed, that light was rendered far less complexly – golden.

'It's really raining here,' Julia said. 'You'll get it soon.'

'No thanks,' I said, 'you can keep it,' realising, after I'd made it, just how often I'd started making this kind of corny non-joke since living with my parents. I hurried the conversation along: 'So, what's new with you?'

'Basically nothing. I've barely done—'

As Julia spoke, I released what I'd anticipated to be a single, deft cough – some minor friction in the throat – but that cough gave way to a larger, consequent cough, then several follow-up coughs trailed after that one.

'Y'okay?'

'Yeah, yeah,' I said, slightly breathless. 'What were you saying?'

'Nothing. I was saying I've done *literally* nothing.'

'Must be nice.'

'No' – a living-room floor lamp momentarily lens-flared into view behind Julia as she shook her head – 'it's really not. Plus Ma can't leave me alone for more than five minutes.'

'I can relate,' I said.

In addition to us having the shared experience of formerly having dated one another, Julia and I had also both been furloughed from our jobs and had recently moved back into our parents' homes.

Admittedly, I had moved months before the pandemic in order to save my way out of my overdraft by avoiding paying rent, while Julia had moved during the pandemic out of immediate necessity: the day after her furloughing, her flatmate – a friend of her older sister's – had evicted her in favour of a new boyfriend she'd met via a dating app, with whom she'd wanted to lock down as a couple.

Since being furloughed, I spent my days working on my writing and nights watching prestige television dramas with my parents, not-drinking alcohol and getting replacement-addicted to the cans of flavoured seltzer water they kept around the house.

Julia, by the sounds of things, had not been having so easy a time. She continued, in a lowered voice: 'It's honestly, like, nightmare-level stuff. Either she's asking me to bake and cook, or she's sniping at me for eating all the time, *or* she's comparing me to my sister.' She put on a nasally, harridan voice: '*Don't you want to get married? Aren't you planning on having children?*'

'Can't you just, like, barricade yourself in your room?'

'No, because then she'll know I'm upset. And when she knows I'm upset' – I noticed Julia was gradually drawing her smartphone toward her face as she spoke – 'she gets even *clingier*. And then, just when I think she can't get any clingier than that, she *outclings* herself someway. Like, the other day, I told her I was going for a walk on my own? But when I got back, she guilted me into looking at old photo albums for an hour – like we had to make up for the time we'd spent apart.'

'God, yeah, I get that too,' I said, which wasn't true at all; my parents were exceptionally thoughtful when it came to giving me space.

'It's just so depressing to think I'm only capable of loving her when we're a four-hour train ride apart.'

'So, you're not especially enjoying being home?'

'Not especially, no. Are you?'

'Oh, yeah. It's fine.'

'And, you've been there for, what, a year now?'

'No-no,' I kneejerk-replied, 'like, nowhere near that long,' before realising, with a shudder, I in fact had been living with my parents for almost that exact amount of time – in my head, I only ever rounded down to when lockdown had started. 'Wait, no, yeah, you're right. A year. More than that, even.'

'And it'll be another year until you're allowed out!'

'Ha ha,' I said, flatly, 'but who's counting.'

'It won't be really another year,' Julia said, seemingly to comfort us both.

'No, I know.'

'But it'll definitely be, like, some months.'

'Right.'

'It is weird, time-wise,' Julia said, 'as in, it's hard to tell how long things've even been going on like this for. D'you find that weekends seem to come around a lot more often nowadays?'

'Yeah,' I said, 'I do find that,' although, in the moment, I struggled to articulate exactly how the pandemic had altered my sense of time's passing.

If I'd written about it, I might have written that the daily density of world-changing events – crossed with the comparative scarcity of the kinds of routine personal micro-experiences that'd formerly set the pace of our lives – had caused our collective perception of time to simulta-neously contract and dilate: hours now felt like days, days felt like weeks; but somehow, months also felt like weeks, and weeks like long afternoons. The recent past seemed further behind us than it really was, while the future had been indefinitely postponed. We were stranded in an eter-nal present.

Televised and livestreamed nightly briefings from government officials compounded this strange sense of atemporality; talking heads veered cautiously away from ever referring to any specific time frames. Instead, time was being managerially reclassified, simplified down to 'the meantime' and 'the foreseeable'; two vague place-holder temporalities that referred only to the non-specific present and proximate future – relegating anything beyond those limited tenses into non-time; into never.

Back in narrative time, Julia changed the subject: 'And, what else? Have you been reading much lately, or no?'

'Yeah,' I said, 'mostly classics,' which sounded affected but was in fact true. I had been almost exclusively reread-ing critical editions of canonical novels I'd first read for my literature degree, along with an accompanying syllabus of photocopied secondary texts from seminars – pretty much all entry-level Freud or excerpts from Norton anthologies – which my parents had kept boxed up in the attic since my graduation. I listed some of the titles I'd recently read, plus a few that I'd been meaning to but still hadn't, then returned the question.

'Don't laugh, but my ma's gotten me into these really lame, like, family sagas.'

'That doesn't sound lame at all.'

'Oh my god, if you don't think it sounds lame, you've clearly never read any. Like, I'm honestly actually ashamed of myself for having gotten so invested in these dumb characters' stupid lives.'

Being extremely lonely, I laughed disproportionately hard at this; hard enough for my chin to double slightly, which I noticed in the picture-in-picture window of my face displaying onscreen, then abruptly ceased laughing.

In the silence that followed my laughter, my thoughts doubled back to the sore subject of my living situation: the grown-up parody of my childhood I mostly avoided ever thinking about too hard.

What would Freud make, I wondered, of my regression into a familial role I should've vacated years before; my failure to properly outgrow the nest I should've left empty as a teenager; the fact that grown adults my own age were, statistically, far likelier to live with their parents than a romantic partner?

I leant my smartphone against my desk lamp and rubbed my eyes with the heels of my palms.

'Are you lost in thought?'

'No, just lost in—' I snuck in a quick *ahem*, '—tired. I've been super-tired lately.'

Then I broke into an extended bout of dry-coughing, after which Julia made big eyes and said, 'Oh my god,' mostly joking, 'd'you think you've got it?'

'I don't have a temperature,' I said, knowing full well, from the many night hours I'd spent patrolling different subreddits dedicated to the virus, that its symptoms varied widely among the afflicted – that not all those with coughs developed fevers; not all those with fevers developed coughs; that many would recover without ever having detected they'd been sick.

This was not to say I didn't think I had the virus (which, naturally, I'd already self-diagnosed as having), but, rather, that – despite initial infection-rate models projecting some eighty per cent of the nation's populace would eventually be sickened by the disease – it still seemed somehow overdramatic to count myself as being among the sickened. 'I'm sure I'm fine,' I said, 'it's been like this for a couple of days. Just gets worse in the evenings.'

'Yeah, if it was going to kill you, it would've by now,' Julia said, with a clear-headedness I appreciated, even though multiple preprint epidemiological case studies available online directly refuted her assertion. 'But are you feeling okay enough to carry on talking?'

'Yep. I'm A-okay.'

'Glad you're A-okay,' she said, smiling and yawning at the same time, 'I'm A-okay, too.'

I told Julia I was glad she was A-okay, retrieved my smartphone from my desk and crossed my room to lie in an attitude of repose on my bed.

Once settled, I wondered aloud what would happen to the expensive seafood restaurant Julia had been working at up until its closure in the interests of public health.

She told me that, while its payrolled staff had all been furloughed and would receive four-fifths of their next few months' salaries, she had her doubts, more generally, about how the industry at large would recover after the virus's suppression: 'Like, so many small- to medium-sized places are going to get shut down.'

While Julia lectured me about the future of the hospitality sector, I quickly navigated away from our FaceTime to refresh my email inbox and send a text – behaviour I found appalling when exhibited by others, but seemingly had no issues with exhibiting myself.

'Are you listening, are you there?' Julia said.

'Yeah,' I said, responding only to the second half of her question; swiping my way back through multiple open apps to resume our conversation. 'Sorry, continue.'

'I was just saying: that place where I worked a while ago might never reopen.'

'That sucks,' I said, automatically, not knowing which place she was referring to. The one with her ex-boyfriend?

'Yeah,' she said, 'but I made proper friends there too.' She adjusted the position of her smartphone slightly, which momentarily freeze-framed her face, prompting another audiovisual delay. 'I don't know. Anyway, I might be quitting cheffing soon and getting into something more normal.'

'Don't do that, you're a great chef,' I said, assuredly, to which Julia replied, 'You've never even been to a restaurant I've cheffed at,' which, after pausing to think about it, I realised was in fact true.

'Well, you made us dinner a few times, way back when,'

I said, although, I remembered now, those meals were mostly all just nice tries; Julia hadn't gotten seriously into cooking until after we'd broken up. 'And it was always great,' I added, too late.

'Gee, thanks,' Julia said.

I coughed again, and recalled having read online that coughing was among the most commonly manifested psychosomatic symptoms of anxiety – this recollection seemed only to further aggravate my coughing.

'Sorry,' I said, after my coughing had subsided, 'I just needed to get that out of my' – before coughing once more – 'system.'

Onscreen, Julia appeared horrified.

'You should see your face,' I said.

'I can see my face,' she said.

I made a mental note to save up my next cough, to time it with a future bout of technical interference.

Then Julia again voiced her concern for my well-being and I zoned fully out of our conversation and started mentally reviewing the last few times I'd been out in public space, amid sites of potential pathogen exposure.

A strange side-effect of the virus – or rather, of the dynamics of its transmission – was the way it had illuminated anew, and with forensic-UV-light intensity, the many overlapping points of interpersonal contact that unified us as a public: how we were all constantly exchanging respirable microdroplets; how we were all constantly touching surfaces others had touched; how we were all (after touching those other-touched surfaces) constantly touching our own faces.

Handshake; junk mail; recyclable plastic packaging – overnight, the formerly commonplace had become the potential vector for disease-spread; the once-familiar now abruptly malign, uncanny (in Freud: 'unheimlich'), a sudden new access of risk.

Trending search terms revealed our concerns about these accesses: how long can the virus survive on plastic? On cardboard? Define: herd immunity. How are contacts traced? Can we flatten the curve? What if the unthinkable befalls someone I love? Might I have, unconscionably, relayed the virus into my parents' home via my trips to the supermarket?

Given their ages and associated levels of immunocompromisation, I had, early on, designated myself as our family's lone grocery gatherer – the deputised adult of the household.

Embarrassing to admit, but it'd been the wide, grey sight of empty supermarket shelves that first impressed upon me a sense of the virus's true magnitude; cornering my shopping cart into a depleted dry-goods aisle, *this* was the moment at which the pandemic-as-hyperobject became real, that I felt the crisis fitting into (then quickly far exceeding) any sense of relative proportion to the rest of the things in my life.

Embarrassing, but: upon exiting the supermarket, I experienced a rapid shortening of breath and had to lean, for a period of minutes, against the driver's-side door of my father's Volvo (on which I'd been temporarily, exorbitantly insured) to commence freaking out about everything that was newly foreseeable: supply-chain fragility; economic collapse; death-toll surges; society coming apart at the seams. Would I asphyxiate here?

I did not asphyxiate there. After the feeling in my chest had been absorbed by the rest of my body, I drove home in silence (with the groceries, for some reason – it'd seemed sensible at the time – seatbelted into the front passenger seat beside me), my facemask lowered like a chinstrap beard, closely monitoring the rate of my breathing; bracing, half-seriously, for death.

'Did you hear what I just said?' Julia said.

'Sure-sure,' I said. Then: 'No. Sorry. I was thinking about the supermarket.'

'Well,' she laughed, 'go ahead and think about the supermarket while you can. Because soon we'll all be' – our connection timed out, autotuning Julia's voice so the word 'be' elongated across several roboticised-sounding syllables, overwriting the next few words she spoke – 'each other, like those creeps in *The Road*' – our connection stabilising – 'remember, in the chapter with the cannibals?'

'Yeah,' I said, 'so crazy, reading that part,' a white but pointless lie; I could, in fact, only remember watching the cannibal scene in *The Road*'s 2009 film adaptation, never having read the novel, despite listing it earlier among the books I'd finished during lockdown.

Julia stared at me dead-eyed for a second and I imagined she'd somehow caught on to my lie – then, several increasingly tense seconds later, I realised our connection had dropped out again.

'Hello?' I said, then repeated, louder; her face still unmoving. 'Fucking Christ.'

'Hi?' she said, our connection returning just soon enough for me to feel like my getting annoyed at its loss had been an overreaction. 'Are you—'

'Say that again?' I said. 'Say again what you were saying?' No response. 'Could you go somewhere with better reception?'

'What?'

'Could you possibly find somewhere with better signal?' I said, then sighed.

'Sure,' she said, moving her smartphone again, its video stream deinterlacing into a series of stop-motion pulses, strobes; 'one second,' carrying our conversation through to her childhood bedroom, affording me a glimpse into its pocket universe: its low, old-house ceiling; hand-embroidered curtains; *Romeo + Juliet* poster; wallpaper frieze depicting a parade of anthropomorphic woodland creatures.

I recalled having, years ago, taken up a fold-out bed in the study directly abutting that room for two separate week-long stretches during the academic calendar's summer and winter breaks; how I'd waited up, nightly, for Julia to knock on our shared wall, signalling that the coast was clear for us to defy the terms of the sleeping arrangement her mother had set. 'Nice room,' I said.

'Ha?' Julia said, flat on her back with her smartphone upraised; its camera angled straight down at her face; a POV shot of you, the viewer, lying on top of her. Funny to think we were both on our beds in our parents' houses, separately, more than a hundred miles apart.

'*Nice room,*' I repeated, placing equal stress on both words. 'Here, I'll show you mine,' I said, toggling from my face-facing camera to my outward-facing one, slowly sideways-panning my smartphone to capture a bed's-eye panorama of my room, unintentionally revealing – I realised, several seconds into shot – a full view of my legs clad in the skintight thermal base-layer bottoms I'd worn unchangingly for the past three days. I quickly flipped the camera back around to show my face.

'Are you wearing long johns?' Julia said, the screen

275

tight around her eyes and nose from where she'd tried to get a closer look.

'Yeah,' I said, 'I put them on special.'

'It's almost summer.'

'Cold here.'

'Maybe you sh—' – her voice again phasing into a metallic blare – 'some online shopping.' She drew her head back into her pillow in surprise. 'Did something happen? Can you see me?'

'Yeah,' I said, 'in, like, VHS-tape quality.'

'Sorry.'

'It's fine,' I said, pulling a mock-annoyed face that Julia didn't seem to notice.

'So, who've you heard from lately?' she said. 'Anyone good?'

Omitting the fact that Julia herself was probably the person I'd heard from the most during lockdown so far, I mentioned one of the recent group Zoom meetings I'd attended with Roos, Teddy and other former university friends – hangouts which, admittedly, always felt like a formality; something we only did to keep up our average number of social events.

Any concerns I might've had about upsetting Julia with news of a Zoom she hadn't been invited to were shortly allayed when she said, 'But, Nick, I asked if you'd heard from anyone *good*.'

'Funny,' I said. 'Y'know, Roos was asking after you.'

'Oh yeah?'

'Yeah. The other day. She thinks you're ignoring her.'

'I'm not ignoring her. What'd she say?'

'Hold on,' I said, 'let me find it, one second,' thumbing my way away from our FaceTime call toward my message inbox; backscrolling through mine and Roos's historical stream of texts. 'Alright, so, this was a couple of weeks ago now. She said: *Have you talked to Julia recently*, and I said: *Yeah*, and she said: *Nice*, and I said: *Yeah*, and she said: *How is she*, and I said: *Fine*.' For what felt like the thousandth time tonight, I cleared my throat. 'Then she said: *Haven't heard from her in forever, she never returns my texts. Is she officially ignoring me?* and I said: *Doubt she is*, and then I added: *Intentionally*, and then I said: *She's probably just stressed with work stuff*, and she said: *Yeah, but we're all stressed with work stuff*, and I said: *True that*, and she said: *Feels sort of like she's mad at me but idk for what reason.* And then we talked about something else.'

'I'm not mad at her,' Julia said.

'I never said you were,' I said, wisely, like I'd pulled off some kind of therapist's trick.

'But, it has been a while since we last spoke. I think, maybe, just, like, the longer you don't talk to someone for, the harder it gets to pick up where you left off.'

'Sure,' I said, 'although, didn't you and I do that? Isn't that exactly what we're doing right now?'

'I mean, yeah,' Julia said. 'But also, no. I don't know. This is different. Besides, university was a long time ago.' Her next words sounded carefully chosen: 'Sometimes people just grow apart.'

There was a distant knocking sound, at which Julia hoisted herself up to sit a little straighter on her bed, looked off-camera and (voice separating from face slightly) sang, 'Five minutes, Ma,' then returned her attention to me.

I asked, 'How's your mother?'

'Apart from annoying? She's fine. Sad church is cancelled. How's yours?'

'Good,' I said, 'Dad's fine too,' remembering again, now, to worry about maybe having transmitted the virus into my parents' home.

'Hey, I was wondering,' Julia said, her face onscreen briefly compressing into a lower resolution.

I raised my eyebrows like: *Go on*.

'How's your writing going? Have you finished anything new?'

'Nothing finished, nothing new,' I said, thinking about the last few stories I'd attempted, which all now read like irrelevant period pieces, set in a frivolous, pre-contagion reality; how much time I'd wasted writing fiction no one would ever read while the world collapsed around me. 'It's just a hobby, anyway,' I added, which was true, although I was surprised to hear myself say it.

'Well, hobbies are good, though. They keep you from going insane.'

'Right.'

'Like, the nice thing about cooking,' Julia said, 'is it gets me out of my head. Otherwise I'd be going fully—' Then her video feed went dark and I lay there in silence, blinking at my smartphone.

'You there?' I said, and received only a skipping and fragmented response.

I hung up and redialled Julia's number, this time as an audio-only call, which I was glad to do – could never quite get acclimated to FaceTiming; could never quite get over the fourth-wall-breaking distraction of being able to see my own face onscreen. The best parts of any conversation, I thought, were those brief stretches of absorption when you were able to forget yourself and feel, in some way, bodiless.

I put the call on loudspeaker and rested my smartphone on my chest as it rang.

'Hello?' Julia answered.

'Yo,' I said.

'I don't know what happened.'

'Your mother lives in a reception dead-spot, is what happened.'

'You were saying something, though? About your writing?'

'No, you were saying. About your cooking.'

'Oh, right, yeah, no. Nothing. I can't remember.'

'Are you looking forward to going back, though? To cooking professionally?'

'No, actually. Like I was saying before, I'm kind of thinking about starting this new thing.'

'Uh-huh. I didn't know—' A weird ring to the way she'd said *starting this new thing*. 'Wait, d'you mean you've already got something lined up?'

'I think so, yeah. For my— Well, I don't want to jinx it while I'm still planning things out.'

'Now you have to say.'

Julia laughed. 'I'm not sure. I really haven't told anyone yet.'

I was going to take the hint and redirect our conversation elsewhere until she added, 'Because it's quite big news,' which I knew meant she was willing to share more information.

'Alright,' I said, 'let's hear.'

'Okay, so' – excitement mounting in her voice – 'y'know my sister lives in Toronto, and has her baby?'

I did know, because Julia had been forwarding me photos of her sister dandling the baby around for weeks.

'Well, I'm planning on heading out there. To Toronto.'

280

'Cool,' I said, 'sounds great.'

'No, like, actually moving there. Just to help with childcare at first, but my sister's hus— My *brother-in-law* says he can eventually get me a job. Apparently his firm's having some big recruitment drive at the end of summer and he's going to hire me for his department. Then I'll be, like, properly living and working in Toronto.'

This news was too unexpected for me to really be upset by it – that would come later – but in the moment, I still knew to deflect away from my gut feeling and pursue a good-natured, highly interested line of questioning. 'Wow, that's—' I began, my voice weak with surprise. 'What kind of job will you get?'

'Oh, just something small in admin or whatever.'

'And, where will you live?'

'My sister's guest room, to start with.'

'And, how long did you say you'll be out there for?'

'I didn't. But, I mean, in theory, maybe the rest of my— Like, I'm pretty much going to restart my whole life there. Crazy, right?'

Branches of hypothetical thought I had allowed – quietly, idly – to open up in my mind over the last few months were now rapidly collapsing away. 'Crazy.'

'This is all visa-dependent, I should add. Hence why I haven't told anyone yet. Not even Ma knows. My sister says there's no point in upsetting her until—'

'Yeah, totally,' I said, only vaguely aware of what I was agreeing with.

'Although, my sister's husband's doing all my visa stuff through his company, which apparently means it's basically a done deal.'

'Crazy,' I said again.

'I know. I just got sick of everything being so up in the air and then I was like: time for something different.' She pivoted tone, her voice now laced with doubt: 'What?'

'I didn't say anything,' I said, suddenly paranoid we'd reverted to FaceTime and Julia could see my expression.

'Exactly. You're *thinking* something.'

'Me? I never think.' I tilted my smartphone upward; relieved to have verified the medium across which our call was taking place. 'But, your plan sounds great.'

'That's nice to hear. I've been dreading telling people.'

'Really great,' I said, nodding, despite being invisible.

'Thanks, Nick,' she said, and exhaled into her smartphone's receiver – audible, on my end, as white noise.

Several prolonged moments of call-silence passed. Eventually, we both started talking at the same time, then both told each other to go first. Then Julia went first.

'I'm just glad we've been talking throughout this whole, y'know. Thing.'

'Same.'

'Because it feels like we've really gotten—'

'Yeah,' I said, a little quicker than I'd intended, but relieved to have spared myself from whatever gently-rejective thing Julia was going to say next. 'This's been good. I'm happy for you. Really.'

'Well. It's still all a long way off. I mean, the actual move won't go ahead for months.'

'Right,' I said, unable to help myself holding on to hope, 'and who knows what'll happen between now and then? You might even end up not going.' As soon as I'd said this, I intuited – with clairvoyant-like surety – that Julia and I would not speak again for some time; for the full duration of the foreseeable.

I saw all our recent communication now for what it was: not a means to starting something new, but a way of tying up loose ends.

I tried to think of a good, non-dramatic conversation closer that could get us both off the hook of having to talk any further.

Eventually, we said some procedural goodbyes with a light-heartedness I was pretty sure neither of us actually felt. These last few moments seemed endless in my experiencing of them, but after we'd hung up, it felt like our call had ended far too quickly.

The new silence that spanned my room seemed also to have made it darker – only now that the call was over did I become fully aware night had fallen. No lights were on around me; no rain beat against my window.

For a while, I thought about all the important, final things I should've said to Julia. Those thoughts eventually passed.

I tried to imagine what her life might look like in Toronto, but when I imagined Toronto, I couldn't picture anything.

Then I had the feeling that I was breathing too-thin air. I coughed a few times – my cough seeming to worsen; something perhaps astir in the lung, or else just a psycho-somatic symptom.

I rolled over onto my side; my smartphone sliding off my chest and landing face-down on the bed beside me. Despite having just finished using it, I felt an urge to turn over and consult the device – an urge I'd always previously yielded to within moments of its having arisen.

Consciously devoting my attention to the act, I breathed in and out; breathed in and out.

Hard to say exactly which impulse draws you back to the smartphone again and again; impossible to distinguish which behaviours are expressions of which initiating drives. Curiosity, boredom, the will to be entertained. A child's fear of the dark.

Notes

'A Restaurant Somewhere Else' is indebted to the works of William T. Vollmann. In that story, the first line of the subsection 'The UTI' interpolates a sentence from Vollmann's 'Whores for Gloria'. The title of the subsection 'I Am Not Living the Right Life' is appropriated from the title of William H. Gass's story 'We Have Not Lived the Right Life', which first appeared in the *New American Review* in 1969.

'Distraction from Sadness Is Not the Same Thing as Happiness' is a phrase I discovered posted anonymously online in the early 2010s.

'Search Engine Optimisation' contains an observation (re: mailboxes) made by Mark Fisher in his lecture 'No Time', given at the Virtual Futures conference in 2011.

Acknowledgements

I would like to thank Tracy Bohan and Alex Bowler for all their work bringing this book into existence.

Thanks, too, to the editors of *The Stinging Fly* and *Granta* for taking early notice of my writing.

Additional thanks to Eric Chinski, and a final thanks to A. C. and A. E. for their encouragement.